Look what people are saying about Tori Carrington...

"Tori Carrington is an unparalleled storyteller with an imagination that is absolutely matchless. These authors are extraordinary and have a true gift for putting their own special brand on anything they touch."
—*Rendezvous* on *Private Investigations*

"One of the genre's most beloved authors."
—*Rendezvous*

"Smart, sassy, and sizzling!"
—Robin Peek, *WordWeaving.com*

"Outrageously hot and erotic."
—Diana Tidlund, *WritersUnlimited.com*

"Deliciously delightful..."
—*SimeGen.com*

"A blazing triumph."
—Harriet Klausner

"One of [the] category's most talented authors."
—*EscapetoRomance.com*

Blaze™

Dear Reader,

Part of what we love about writing is the opportunity to immerse ourselves in worlds that are utterly foreign to us. To examine the people who inhabit these places, and ultimately not only understand them and accept that this is their reality, but to come to love them for who they are and root for them.

This has never been more true for us than it was with *Dangerous*.... Gia Trainello is a mafia princess who is elevated to Lady Boss when her father and brother are assassinated, sucked back into a life she left behind a long time ago along with love Lucas Paretti. But Lucas is not what he appears. Gia must find out the hard way that the road to hell is, indeed, paved with good intentions. And that lost love is the ultimate sacrifice.

We hope you're riveted by Gia and Lucas's sometimes heartbreaking journey toward happily-ever-after. We'd love to hear what you think. Contact us at P.O. Box 12271, Toledo, OH 43612 (we'll respond with a signed bookplate, newsletter and bookmark), or visit us on the Web at www.toricarrington.net.

Here's wishing you love, romance and HOT reading.

Lori & Tony Karayianni
aka Tori Carrington

TORI CARRINGTON
Dangerous...

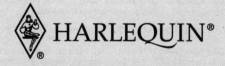

HARLEQUIN®

TORONTO • NEW YORK • LONDON
AMSTERDAM • PARIS • SYDNEY • HAMBURG
STOCKHOLM • ATHENS • TOKYO • MILAN • MADRID
PRAGUE • WARSAW • BUDAPEST • AUCKLAND

ISBN-13: 978-0-373-79363-1
ISBN-10:   0-373-79363-4

DANGEROUS…

www.eHarlequin.com

Printed in U.S.A.

ABOUT THE AUTHOR

Romantic Times BOOKreviews Career Achievement Award winning husband-and-wife duo Lori and Tony Karayianni are the power behind the pen name Tori Carrington. Their more than thirty-five novels include titles for Harlequin Blaze, Harlequin Temptation, Signature and Silhouette Special Edition, as well as their ongoing Sofie Metropolis, PI series for Forge. They call Toledo, Ohio, home base, but travel to Tony's hometown of Athens, Greece, whenever they can. For more information on the couple, their books and where they plan to appear next with a fresh batch of Tony's Famous Baklava in hand, visit www.toricarrington.net.

Books by Tori Carrington

We dedicate this book to all those who ceaselessly strive toward a greater understanding of the world around us and the people who inhabit it. And to our spectacular editor Brenda Chin, who knows what we're trying to say when we're having a hard time saying it.

Prologue

CLAUDIO LANCIONE WAS the last person who would normally attract Gia Trainello. She'd known him for most of her life and he'd always been a part of the family. A fixture, really. Handsome, yes. But she'd never so much as shared a suggestive smile with him, much less a kiss and promise of something more. But grief, it was said, made people do strange things.

And Gia was definitely grieving.

The four-star hotel-room sheets chafed Gia's bare legs as she curled into a ball. Had it really only been four days since her father and younger brother, Mario, had been gunned down in broad daylight? A day since she'd said her final good-byes at a burial service attended by hundreds she hadn't wanted to face? Twenty-four hours since she'd watched her older brother, Lorenzo, being pushed away in a wheelchair, barely conscious of what had happened because his private nurse had given him enough sedatives to make a bull lie down before a matador during his brief excursion from the hospital?

A few hours since she'd slipped Claudio a note asking him to meet her, desperately wanting, needing to feel something other than the pain crowding her chest, making it almost impossible for her to breathe, and then virtually ripping off his clothes the instant he'd entered the hotel suite?

Oh, she'd managed to throw herself into the physical sexual activity. Had even achieved a shallow climax or two. But always, always there were the images of her father's and brother's closed caskets. Always, always there was the memory of the line of nonstop visitors milling through her father's house to offer their condolences and to drink wine from his carefully stocked cellar. Always, always there was the feeling that she no longer belonged in the house where she had grown up and which she had long since left, even though she felt obligated to receive the visitors—especially with Lorenzo—the third victim of the tragedy—still hospitalized.

Always, always there was the gaping hole in her life that she feared might never be filled again.

The image of Luca Paretti claimed her mind's eye. Striking Luca Paretti, standing to the side of the casket, forever present during the reception, reminding her of times better forgotten. Luca Paretti, who had once willingly played young Romeo to her teenage Juliet…and then disappeared when she'd needed him most, only to reappear again a few months ago.

Luca Paretti, the one she truly longed to be in bed with just then even though the two of them hadn't shared more than a few cordial words in four days.

Even if allowing him entrance back into her life and her heart would be the ultimate mistake.

Claudio moved beside her and Gia went still, hoping he hadn't awakened. She just needed a few moments more to herself. A little longer to feel the warmth, however fleeting and deceptive, against her skin before she had to force herself out of the bed and on with the rest of a life that wouldn't include her father, brother…or Luca Paretti.

Her cell phone vibrated on the night table. Gia stared at it, and then the clock next to it: 4:30 a.m. Who would be calling her at such an ungodly hour? Only someone wanting to share ungodly news.

Claudio curved against her backside. "Are you going to get that?"

Gia uncurled her legs and entwined them with his. "I was thinking about it."

The phone went silent and the decision was taken away from her.

Like most decisions over the past few days. Not only in connection to the funeral arrangements. Her interest in her Bona Dea Fashion Designs had been nil and her partner, Bryan Dragomir, had had to step in to fill both pairs of shoes.

She rubbed her forehead with the heel of her hand and closed her eyes. For so long she'd lived outside the cone of the family's influence. While only the East River had separated her from the Venuto crime family, it had seemed like an ocean when she'd originally gone into the city to attend the Fashion Institute of Technology. Farther still when she'd started Bona Dea with her dearest friend, Bryan, spending the past five years building the company into a force to be reckoned with in the New York fashion world. They owned three upscale boutiques in Manhattan and had plans to expand even further, with shops in Chicago, Dallas and L.A.

But the death of her father and brother had sucked her back into the family with the strength of a riptide. Reminding her of the fear she'd had growing up. The worry that her father might be killed had shadowed every moment of every day. And when her two brothers signed on, she'd feared they'd been added to death's list.

A list she'd escaped first because she was a woman, second because Luca Paretti had made it impossible to stay in a place that reminded her forever of him.

But while she'd been aware of the danger that surrounded many of her family members, she'd never expected that they'd all be taken from her in one fell swoop.

Or by one assassin's gun.

And while Lorenzo was still on this side of the earth that covered her father and younger brother, he wasn't walking it. And might never walk it again.

The telephone began to vibrate anew even as she felt Claudio's hand slide around her waist then shift up to cup her breast.

She reached for the phone.

The number was unlisted.

"Hello?"

"Gia?"

"This is she."

"Vito here."

Vito. Her father's second in command. The man who had been as broken as any blood relative by recent events. And had taken care of so much over the past few days when she'd been incapable of seeing too much of anything at all.

"Sorry to call you so late. But I've got some information on the people responsible for the killings. And you said you wanted to know the instant it came in."

That seemed so long ago, when she'd stood over her father's casket and told the man she called Uncle Vito that she wanted revenge.

"I've come up with one name so far. Claudio Lancione."

Gia lay frozen for a full minute, trying to assimilate the information. She didn't question Vito. If he said the man who was stroking her breast even now had been involved in the shooting, then he'd been involved. It was as simple as that.

Her stomach clenched tightly, filling her throat with bile as shame and fury fought for control within her.

"Where are you?" Vito asked. "I want to send a couple of guys to keep an eye on you until we figure out how deep inside the family the conspiracy goes."

Vito apparently understood enough to know that she wasn't at her Upper West Side penthouse apartment. But not enough to know that she was with Claudio right that moment.

She told him where she was and then slowly closed the phone.

"What's going on?" Claudio asked.

Gia swallowed thickly, afraid she might be sick as she gathered her wits tightly around her. "They have the name of one of those responsible for the hit."

He rolled on top of her, his manhood hard and pulsing between her legs. "Oh, yeah? Who?"

Gia arched her back, and stretched her arms above her head, appearing to be doing nothing more than bracing herself against the headboard for another round of sex.

Instead she reached for Claudio's holster where he'd hung it on the far bedpost, her fingers trembling. She kissed him deeply, hot tears blurring his features, even as she freed the gun, blindly sought and found the safety and switched it off, and then brought the cold metal muzzle to rest against Claudio's temple.

"You."

She squeezed the trigger.

1

One month later...

LUCAS PARETTI STOOD off to the side of the wide
front steps to the Long Island Trainello estate,
watching as people came and went, none of them
leaving a particularly lasting impression. It was
at times like these when it was all too easy to
forget the past seven years existed. Too easy to
remember himself as little more than a kid fasci-
nated by, and proud to be associated with, the
family. More specifically, the Venuto crime
family, one of the most powerful of five mafia
families in the New York City area that had been
headed by Giovanni Trainello.

Too easy to imagine that he and Gia Trainello
were the same young couple in love, stealing a
few, precious minutes alone whenever they could.

Then he remembered his younger brother,
Angelo, and he felt the warmth leave his blood.

He fished for a cigarette from a pack he'd had for a month and lit up, squinting through the blue smoke at the street.

Angelo. There was a time when not a moment went by when he wasn't acutely aware of the loss. When he went to his parents' small walk-up Brooklyn apartment and felt that emptiness everywhere he looked, including in his parents' faces, and saw the way they appeared twenty years older than they were.

Angelo had been seventeen when he'd vowed to follow in Lucas's footsteps.

Seventeen when he began going to the Trainello business front in Brooklyn begging for odd jobs.

Seventeen when he'd been gunned down, forever losing his rights to turning eighteen.

Lucas looked down the long, curving driveway bordered by lush, mature trees, suddenly surprised that he was out in Long Island instead of in Brooklyn where his brother had been killed. For a moment he could smell the wet concrete sidewalk that had recently been watered down, the exhaust from cars on a nearby busy street. In his mind's eye, he saw the yellow crime scene tape and the stain made by Angelo's blood.

And the spot on his own shirt, made as he'd

cradled his brother's head in his arms, pleading for him to come back.

The flashbacks didn't happen as often as they once did. Which was a good thing. Because if he thought about what had happened to his brother every moment of every day, he would never be able to function. Never be able to focus on what he had come back to New York, come back into the family, to do.

Another part of him supposed he'd purposely pushed thoughts of his brother aside over the past month because the entire reason for him being there had changed, and by all rights he should have quit his cover position as Venuto family attorney and have been on the first plane back to St. Paul, returning to New York only to occasionally visit his parents.

A black Lexus sedan pulled up the driveway, the reason why he wasn't on that plane and was instead still working undercover sitting in the back seat. Gia Trainello. He took another drag off the cigarette, watching her black stiletto heels hit the pavement, her black stockings clinging against her shapely calves as she got out. Her gaze locked with his beyond her large sunglasses and she looked surprised to see him. Just as she had nearly every day over the past month since her father and brother had been killed.

Then the moment passed and she'd either nod or say hello, and circumstances returned to normal.

"Morning, Luca," she said softly.

"Good morning."

And just like that the driver handed her her bags from the trunk of the car and the connection was broken, restless ghosts chased back into the shadows of the past as she walked up the stairs to the sprawling Italian villa-style estate and disappeared inside the house.

Gia Trainello. The reason why he'd stuck around.

And the number-one reason why he should still catch the first flight out for St. Paul.

THE QUIET MOMENTS in Gia's life were few and far between now. Which wasn't entirely a bad thing. The busier she was, the less likely she was to remember that night at the Seasons when she'd shot Claudio with his own gun and then lay there with his motionless body on top of her until Vito's men arrived. It had taken the sound of them gaining access to the room to bring her around to the reality of the situation. And as soon as they'd removed his body, she'd curled into a fetal position, ignoring attempts to get her to move, to leave the room before anyone started snooping around. Or, worse yet, called the police.

She couldn't remember who had dressed her and taken her back to her place. All she could recall was that when she awakened twelve hours later and clawed her way to the shower, her skin was still covered with Claudio's blood.

And twelve long hours after that, when her known world had refused to start revolving again, and she'd felt the shadows of the Venuto family sucking at her heels, she'd known what she had to do if she hoped to ever return to any kind of sense of normalcy: she had to step into her father's shoes until her father and brother's assassins were brought to justice.

Family justice.

In the past month, her days had come to look very different from the life she'd known before. She'd packed her penthouse apartment in mothballs and then moved back into the family house in Long Island. There wasn't a time when there weren't at least five armed men around her, and more guarding the compound. It was almost as if the past seven years in Manhattan had never existed...except for when her partner, Bona Dea

Bryan, came to visit her to discuss company business.

Like he was this morning.

She stood at the window, watching where Luca spoke to Vito on the back balcony. Luca was smoking a cigarette, which likely explained why the conversation was taking place outside. Longing, pure and strong, swept through her veins. Both for the man now, and the man she'd known in the past.

"Gia? Are you still with me?" Bryan asked from behind her. She turned to face him.

That was the question, wasn't it? Was she still with him? Physically, she was in her father's old-world office, the new designs for the spring collection spread out on a polished oak conference table between the two of them, but emotionally she was far, far away.

"I'm sorry. I missed the last part of what you said."

Bryan sighed. "I don't think you've heard a single word since I arrived an hour ago."

"Don't be silly." She took in his dubious look. "I heard half. At least."

He chuckled and then closed the sketchbook. "That's okay. We can do this another time. I mean, a couple of days isn't going to make that big of a difference."

But she knew that it would. New York Fashion Week was only a month and a half away and it would be then that they would spotlight their spring collection. Which meant important decisions needed to be made. Pieces chosen and rushed into production. Ads taken out. Meetings to arrange. Magazine editors to wine and dine.

Bryan zipped up his case. But rather than kiss her goodbye and leave, he let the case drop back to the table, then gestured for her to sit with him in the chairs facing the fireplace, left cold in the August heat. Gia caressed the arms of the leather wing chair. Her father's favorite.

"I'm worried about you, Gia," Bryan said, watching her closely.

That was a switch. Ever since they'd become fast friends in college, she'd been the one to look after him. Despite his macho demeanor, Bryan was a big softy and she'd often spent time talking him through heartache or an attack of nerves. Their individual strengths shored up the other's weaknesses, making them great business partners. And even better friends.

She managed a smile. "Don't be. I'm fine."

"Are you?"

She averted her gaze. No, she wasn't. But she would be. Soon.

"Are the rumors true?"

"What rumors?"

"That you're the new Lady Boss of the Venuto family."

Gia stared at him, his words at odds with his WASPish good looks and friendly grin.

Of course, it wasn't the first she'd heard the reference. The New York dailies had been running pieces on her for weeks following the funeral, most times with bold headlines calling her the same.

"Don't be ridiculous," she said. "I'm just straightening out some unfinished business."

"Estate matters?"

She didn't answer immediately. Then she said, "Something like that."

"How's your brother?"

Lorenzo. Her heart ached. "Getting better."

Gia wondered when lying had become so easy for her. The truth was that Lorenzo wasn't doing well at all. He'd developed an addiction to the pain pills prescribed to help him deal with his spinal-injury pain. So rather than seeing to the therapy sessions necessary to help him regain his mobility, he passed his days lying in a hospital bed she'd had set up in his old bedroom upstairs, with twenty-four-hour nursing care, and only doctor visits as the highlight of his days.

"Look, Bry," she said, leaning closer to him, "I appreciate your concern. But I'm fine. Really. All this is…just temporary. If you can continue to hold down the fort a little longer without me…I'll be back on the job in no time flat. You just wait and see."

He appeared doubtful. And she couldn't blame him.

Still, he nodded and then looked at his watch. "I've got to get back to the city. I have an eleven o'clock with Elite to close the deal on the models we want for the show."

Gia stood up to give him a hug and a kiss on the cheek. "Thanks for coming out."

He shook his finger at her as he picked up his case from the table. "Next time you come to the office."

Gia walked him to the door, noticing how the armed men blended into the shadows to let him pass. He got into the car he'd hired to bring him out and then disappeared down the driveway.

She turned around to find the last person on earth she needed to see standing behind her. And her throat tightened to the point of pain.

Luca Paretti.

2

LUCAS HAD BEEN WAITING for over an hour for Gia to finish with her meeting. He supposed that was part of the price he paid for expecting to see Gia— now referred to as Miss Gia by family members— without an appointment. But every time he'd called over the past month to book a time when he might talk to her, she'd avoided him at every turn.

So he'd had to push his luck by confronting her when she wasn't expecting it.

"Luca," she said on what might have been a sigh, using the Italian pronunciation of his name rather than Lucas.

"Gia. You look well."

She took his hands and kissed him on both cheeks, but the movement was perfunctory, with no warmth behind the action. At least not the kind of warmth he may have wanted. Despite the way she seemed to linger after the second kiss, as if reluctant to move away from him.

But she did, stepping back so that he could look into her wide, dark eyes.

"Sorry to have to resort to subterfuge to see you," Lucas said, following her to Giovanni's office without waiting to be invited. "But I have several important matters to discuss with the head of the family. And since I understand that title has been bestowed on you, then you're the one I need to discuss them with."

The first time he'd seen her after so many years, he'd felt like someone had hit him in the chest with a two-by-four. While she'd been pretty when he'd known her before, there had been a girl-child innocence about her. Now…well, now she was one hundred percent smoky Mediterranean beauty, whose dark eyes spoke of a mystery and wisdom that surpassed her years.

He'd seen countless pictures of her in the paper in recent weeks. Whether the shots focused on her in a black veil weeping over her father's and brother's caskets, or getting out of a family limousine, she always seemed to be looking elsewhere, her features set in dark determination. An elusive beauty always dressed in black.

And today was no exception. She wore a stylish clingy black top and skinny black pants, the flats she wore making her six inches shorter than him, but still tall by female standards at around five-nine.

Over the years, he'd followed her career from afar and knew that many questioned why she would choose a role behind the fashion scene instead of up front and center. She easily equaled, if not eclipsed, many of the models she used for her shows and print ads.

But the media didn't know what he did about Gia: namely that after her mother died when she was seven, she'd escaped into a world of her own making. A cerebral world of books and art and fashion. And, aside from his few carefree months with her, that's where she remained.

He remembered saying that when he grew up, he wanted to be attorney to the mob, and that she had wanted to be the next Donatella Versace.

He supposed they both got what they'd wanted.

He could tell her she looked good but knew that would have little impact on her. In fact, it might hurt his cause, because she'd likely shut him out. He'd heard the stories about her having seen to the Claudio Lancione hit on her own. Some said that they'd even been having sex at the time. But he couldn't think about that in order to do what he had to.

"What can I do for you, Luca?" she asked, as if she hadn't spent the past month avoiding him.

But he knew she had been avoiding him. Not because she was grieving, although he knew she was. He saw it in the faint circles under her eyes. In the extra paleness of her skin.

But because he had left her without explanation seven years ago.

"There are some legal matters you need to attend to immediately unless you want everything to come crashing down around your ears."

She raised a black brow. "I'm sure Vito can help you with whatever you need."

Lucas shook his head. "No. Only the person in charge can see to these matters."

She held his gaze for a long moment, as if trying to read beyond his actions. He wondered when she'd become so guarded. No, he didn't have to wonder. He knew. And he knew he'd played a role in one of her first understandings that life wasn't all sunshine and daisies and good intentions. Oh, she'd certainly been aware of danger—after all, she'd been born and raised under the Trainello roof. But he'd been among the first to wrong her.

And now she'd been wronged again.

"I'm in charge only until my brother Lorenzo

can take over." She finally broke their gaze and walked toward her father's old desk. He caught the way she ran her fingertips across the top before sitting down in the chair and looking at him again. He took the seat opposite her.

"I understand he's doing better," Lucas said, even though he knew that that wasn't the case at all. Her older brother was little more than a functioning vegetable by choice.

Still, Gia nodded, giving away nothing with her expression as she folded her hands on top of the desk. "What do you need, Luca? I don't have much time."

He opened his briefcase and took out a series of documents. "These are the Trainello estate papers. I assume that you'd like to be named power of attorney. You know, until Lorenzo can take over."

She nodded.

"Well, you have to do that legally. There have already been several claims made against the estate having to deal with outstanding debt and the like that you'll have to see to. And, of course, there's probate that you'll have to go through."

He put the papers in front of her.

"Can't someone else do all this?" she asked.

"Yes," Lucas said. "Me. But you'd have to sign that power over to me."

Finally, a show of emotion via a spark in her dark eyes. "I'm not signing any power over to anyone."

Lucas sat back, mildly amused. "That's what I thought you'd say. Which means you need to sign where I've indicated. You won't have to do much. I'll take care of overseeing what needs to be done...with your supervision, of course."

She finally appeared to give the papers in front of her the attention they deserved.

Lucas fought the urge to tug at his collar. In all his imaginings, he would never have thought that being in Gia's company again after so long would bring back a few memories of his own. Or inspire in him a desire to relive a great many of them.

Despite what his actions might have left her to believe, she'd touched a place inside him no one else had been able to reach. And even now that spot ached in a way he was helpless to stop.

At least not in her presence.

He cleared his throat and started to get up. "Why don't I just leave the documents with you and come back for them."

She blinked at him, apparently surprised by his abrupt change in behavior. Hadn't he been the one to insist on the meeting? Why, then, was he in a hurry to get out of there?

She sighed. "Fine."

She put the papers aside and then rose to lead him to the door.

Lucas followed. "How about dinner?"

She looked at him so quickly a strand of her shiny, long black hair stuck to her red lips. "What?"

"Dinnertime," Lucas explained, watching as she put the strand back into place.

One simple move. One tiny blip in time. One undeniable distraction that switched his mind from the matter at hand to the woman who was close enough to touch.

He breathed in the smell of her perfume. A subtle mixture of lemon and vanilla. It was all he could do not to lean in closer so he might get a better sense of how the scent mingled with her own personal aroma.

He quietly cleared his throat, but the act did little to return his voice to normal. "Why don't I come back around dinnertime. Surely you take time out to eat, don't you? I can collect the papers then and talk to you about other matters at hand."

Gia apparently caught on to his attentive state and his preoccupation with the pulse at the base of her neck where he imagined she'd applied her perfume this morning. She swallowed thickly even as her pupils grew large.

Lucas was powerless to stop his mouth from moving toward where hers loomed temptingly within reach.

"Miss Gia?" one of the Trainello goons that had been hiding in the shadows emerged, wearing an earpiece he was apparently listening to. "Your next appointment has arrived."

The connection snapped.

Lucas squared his shoulders and Gia took a physical step away.

"Very good, Tony," she said, louder than necessary. "Um, escort Mr. Tamburo into the library until I call for him."

She turned back toward Lucas, looking mystified by him, bewildered by her own emotions.

And—he hoped—perhaps on a level she was loath to admit, still anticipating his kiss.

"How's six o'clock?" he asked.

She looked toward where Tony had been a moment before and then back at him. He fully expected her to refuse the dinner meeting.

Instead, she met his gaze head-on and said, "Make it seven."

Lucas watched her make her way back down the hall, appearing more self-conscious of her movements than she had been before.

Then he turned, opening the front door at the

same time as Vincenzo Tamburo, the head of the Peluso crime family, climbed the last step, two of his henchman in tow.

Whatever lingering emotions might have remained after nearly kissing Gia vanished instantly, yanking him soundly back to the reality of the here and now.

Lucas gave the other man a nod and the mafia don nodded back.

Christ.

Vincenzo Tamburo headed the second most powerful crime family in the city and was not a man to be taken lightly even when he was smiling, as he was doing now. He was ruthless and deadly, known to go to any and all lengths to keep his power intact. It was said that last year he'd had his own son-in-law whacked, the man's body found at a Queens dump site, while his severed head had never been recovered. It was rumored that Tamburo had it preserved in a jar in his safe to remind himself that he could trust no one.

The son-in-law's crime? Taking some initiative in his new role in the family and making his father-in-law a fortune from a Brinks-truck robbery that Tamburo hadn't authorized.

Lucas stared at the older man's wide back.

Jesus, he hoped Gia knew what in the hell she was getting herself into.

And he hoped that when all was said and done, he would be able to protect her from the worst of it.

3

AN HOUR LATER, Gia stood at the French doors of her father's office, trying to soothe her nerves by rubbing her hands up and down her bare arms. It wasn't that her meeting with Tamburo hadn't gone as expected. It had. What she hadn't anticipated was that the overbearing man would shake her to the core with his leering stares and arctic smiles.

She'd suspected that her familiar connection to her father's old "friends" would change somewhat for the duration she sat at the helm. After all, she'd known these men all her life and they had been like uncles to her, providing her with lavish birthday gifts, big bear hugs and enthusiastic cheek pinches. They were probably as surprised as she was by her new title, however temporary. At worst, she'd allowed that perhaps they'd try to treat her like that child they'd watched grow up.

She'd never expected Uncle Vincenzo to look

at her as if he'd prefer to see her hanging from a meat hook.

The question was, could Vincenzo Tamburo have given the order to pull the trigger of the gun that took her father's life?

"Romulus! Stop!"

Gia blinked the backyard into focus. Or, more precisely, she watched as a hundred pounds of lean, mean Bucciuriscu canine lumbered onto the patio outside the doors she stood in front of, covered in soapsuds.

"Come back here right now, you," a guy that was more gangly teen than man demanded as he followed the stubborn dog.

Romulus's red tongue rolled out of his mouth in a doggie grin as he considered his pursuer and then proceeded to shake off the suds, covering the teen and the doors, causing even Gia to take a step back.

"Oh, Romulus, you no good hound," the kid said in exasperation. "If you were my dog, I'd be having you for supper."

Gia smiled for what felt like the first time in months. Romulus was one of two of her father's purebreds, the other, Remus, of course, after the infamous mythological Roman twins.

She watched as Romulus planted himself,

making it impossible for the kid to budge him from the patio.

Gia opened the soap-speckled doors. The kid looked up at her, having to shield his eyes from the sun. "Oh, God. I'm sorry, Miss Gia. I didn't see you there." He grimaced. "You didn't hear what I said, did you?"

"What's your name?"

"Fusco, ma'am. Frankie Fusco."

"Please, just call me Gia."

She bent over and stroked the snout of the hulking guard dog.

"Yes, Miss Gia." Frankie tugged on a handful of fur at the back of Romulus's neck and nearly lost his fingers to the dog in the process.

"No, he won't do anything for you that way," she said. "Buccuriscus are highly aggressive dogs. You have to show them who's boss." She whistled for Romulus's attention and then snapped her fingers, pointing to her side. "Here, Romy."

The dog instantly obeyed, coming to stand next to her.

"Sit."

He sat.

She patted the back of his wet head. "Where are you washing him?"

"Out by the garage, Miss Gia."

That meant that Frankie had chased the dog a good ways around the grounds. Not surprising.

"Just Gia," she said again.

"I couldn't call you by your first name, Miss Gia. It wouldn't be showing you the proper respect."

Respect definitely had its drawbacks.

"You try commanding him," she suggested.

Frankie followed her lead.

Romulus barked once at him and stayed put.

And then he stood again and shook himself out, spraying Gia with whatever suds and water remained on his thick fur.

She and Frankie looked at each other and laughed.

"Come on," Gia said. "Now that I'm dressed for the job, I might as well help you out."

"Oh, no, Miss Gia." Frankie looked stricken. "I couldn't ask you to do that."

"Are you disobeying an order, Fusco?"

"Me? Oh, no. No, I wouldn't dream of it."

"Come on, then."

Gia ordered Romy to heel at her side and she and Frankie walked the span of lawn behind the house toward the garage.

"How long you been working here?" Gia asked.

"Two months tomorrow, Miss Gia."

"And your duties?"

He reached down to pat Romy, who growled at him threateningly. He snatched his hand back. "Well, washing the dogs. Running errands for the guys. Stuff like that."

"Do you like it?"

"Like it? I love it. I've been trying to work for the family for years."

Gia smiled at his exaggeration. He couldn't be more than a day over eighteen.

"I was bussing tables at the Guarinos' and running numbers when I met your father, God rest his soul." He looked awkward about mentioning her dad. "My condolences, Miss Gia."

"Thank you."

"Anyway, I met your father and he brought me out here to see to some things. I stay in the stables with the other guys."

Gia looked toward the converted stables in question that were barely visible through a thatch of trees and flowering bushes, and then turned back toward Frankie. She could see why her father had been taken with the teen. He didn't appear to have an insincere bone in him. His obvious youth aside—she'd met more eighteen-year-olds who looked forty than she could count

over the past month—he was open and enthusiastic and apparently relished his connection to the
family.

Of course, she'd seen much of the same mis-
placed interest growing up. Especially from the
kids who came up in the area of Brooklyn that the
Venuto family had controlled since Prohibition.
Where teens in other neighborhoods might join
gangs, in the Venuto neighborhood, the family
was the gang. And, it seemed, every kid wanted
to be a member.

They rounded the corner of the garage to find
one of Vito's goons standing in shirtsleeves in the
summer heat, his shoulder holster and firearm
clearly visible. Romulus's brother, Remus, sat
quietly waiting his turn for a bath.

"Romy, sit," Gia ordered.

The dog whined at her and then did as she asked.

"Thanks, Miss Gia," Frankie said, appearing
not to know what to do. He held out his hand to
shake hers, and then stared at where it was
covered in suds and drew it quickly back. "I'm
sorry to have disturbed you."

"No bother," Gia said, looking around. She'd
have to ask Vito to have his men cover their
weapons.

Just as she thought his name, she spotted Vito

at the edge of the part of the driveway leading to the garage, speaking to a man she didn't recognize. Of course, she had yet to name all of the personnel around the sprawling estate, but she was pretty sure she hadn't seen this guy before.

She watched as the two men shook hands, and then the dark stranger rounded the front of a BMW sedan and climbed inside. Moments later, he disappeared down the long driveway toward the road.

Frankie looked as if he had things well in hand, so she began making her way back toward the office's back entrance.

She turned slightly. "Frankie?"

He immediately snapped to attention, the soapy sponge he held covering his face in suds. He wiped them away with the back of his hand.

"How would you like a promotion to personal assistant?"

LUCAS LET HIMSELF into the small studio apartment he'd rented in Queens, careful to avoid being seen. Of course, that he'd left his car on Queens Boulevard, changed into a tracksuit, Mets cap and athletic shoes in a subway bathroom, and then caught the next train to the apartment had helped in his subterfuge.

He threw the five different locks on the door

and flicked on the one light in the cramped space. There was only a sofa bed, a desk and a small kitchen and bathroom. The walls bore peeling wallpaper that revealed a different pattern wallpaper underneath. The floorboards beneath his shoes were scratched and gouged, multiple coats of paint having come up over the years.

He tossed his keys onto the desk and shrugged out of the track jacket, removing the palm-size tapes he'd put in the pockets and staring at them. They represented more than thirty hours of conversations he'd had over the past week. One with Gia, herself.

Sitting down in an old wooden chair, he considered the tapes, dumping the ones that held conversations with Vito and other family members into one shoe box, the last tape that included today's conversation with Gia into another.

Like clockwork, the cell phone that he left in the apartment rang.

He picked up on the second ring.

"What have you got?" his FBI handler asked.

"Not much. Things have been quiet."

Silence. Then, "How are you going in your effort to get closer to Gia Trainello?"

Lucas rubbed his forehead. His handler even asking the question made him feel like dirt.

Yes, the bureau knew the rumors that Gia had taken over in her brother's stead. And he'd been ordered to get closer to her. His handler didn't know his past with the onetime mafia princess. And if he had any say in it, he wouldn't, either. What had happened between him and Gia seven years ago was between them. Period. It didn't enter into his current job assignment. Which, simply, was to bring down the Venuto crime family, and possibly any other families he could along with them.

Still, he said, "I've established contact in order to discuss estate papers."

"And?"

"And that's it."

Lucas leaned back in the chair, causing it to creak, a part of him daring his handler to press him for more information.

Damn it. He should have asked to be reassigned the moment Giovanni and Mario Trainello were hit. Forget the years' worth of tapes and wiretaps and his hands-on investigation into the crime organization.

But he hadn't asked. Because every time he'd thought about doing so, he remembered Angelo. Recalled his younger brother's pale face against the satin that lined his casket. And that alone was enough to remind him that what he was doing now was the culmination of seven years of hard work. Any day now, he would have the revenge he'd craved for the better half of his adult life.

He would see to it that the family responsible for his brother's death paid the ultimate price for its crimes.

Gia...

A small voice whispered her name in the back of his mind.

Of course, he'd try to protect Gia any way he could. He was determined to keep her out of it, both because of their past together...and because she didn't deserve to be hurt by him again.

But if push came to shove...

Well, he'd have to wait until it came to that.

4

LATER THAT EVENING, a while after Luca had gone following dinner, Gia bent over the additional papers he had left with her, trying to concentrate on the words instead of trying to interpret the meaning of his actions.

It had been so long ago that she'd been in love with him. But not so long that she couldn't remember what it was like to look at him and feel something larger than herself expand within her. Experience a desire that made her feel like she might combust if she couldn't kiss his mouth, feel the cool texture of his hair under her fingertips.

Luca represented a time in her life when all was good. When family was family and when one look into his eyes had been enough to make her smile for a week.

But that time was long past. No matter how much a part of her wanted to believe differently.

And if she needed any reminder of that fact, all she had to think about was what happened after he'd left. What she had gone through alone that had left a jagged scar across her soul that could never be forgotten.

She unfolded her legs from under her on the overstuffed couch in the library and walked to the French doors, staring out into the deep summer night. A shadow moved and she started, still not used to having armed men around in order to protect her. She hadn't needed them in seven years.

She needed them now.

But rather than their presence making her feel safe, she felt as if she was imprisoned. The reminder that danger lurked everywhere unnerving.

What did Luca want? Oh, she'd known the instant he'd come back to New York a year ago and rejoined the family as one of the lead attorneys. It had been all her father had talked about at the time. Luca had been his golden boy years earlier, second only after Lorenzo, rating a spot even before headstrong Mario. Luca was a man who instilled trust in others and was more than capable of seeing any assignment through to the end.

The description had been her father's. She hadn't asked what he'd meant by "any assignment." She hadn't wanted to know.

What she did want to know was what Luca had done while he was gone.

And why he'd left the city after his younger brother had been killed during a random mugging.

Was it the tragedy of losing his brother? Was that why he'd left?

But his parents had remained in Brooklyn. Gia had even visited them. Once.

She'd never gone back again.

After everything that had happened since, every ounce of common sense told her that she shouldn't care why Luca had left, what he had done while he was gone, and why he was back now.

But, God help her, she did care.

She absently rubbed her arm. While it was still August hot outside, the air-conditioned temperature inside was kept low. Just as her father had liked it. And she hadn't had the heart yet to change even the thermostat.

The trivial detail brought a memory flooding back as if it could have happened yesterday instead of nearly twenty years ago.

It had been a cold, rainy March day. Most of the mourners had left the grave and her grandmother was in the waiting limousine with her brothers. She and her father were all who remained.

Holding her father's hand, the new patent-leather shoes her grandmother had bought her sinking into the mud, Gia had watched as the shiny mahogany casket had been lowered into the ground. The top had been covered with yellow roses, her mother's favorite. Gia had felt numbed by her emotions and the weather.

"She looks lonely," she'd said.

Her father had blinked then, as if he'd been in a trance, and looked down at her, his hand squeezing hers. "She's with family now." He looked up at the rain-soaked skies. "In heaven."

"But we're family."

Her father had stood for a long moment, staring down at her. Then he'd crouched so that they were close to eye level. "Yes, *piccina,* we are family. But the family in heaven needed your mommy more than we did."

Gia had spotted the pain on his face even as he said the words and had wondered if he was comforting her or himself.

"I miss her."

Gia wasn't sure if it was the rain trailing down his handsome face or tears as he enveloped her in a hug, holding her tight, holding her close. "I do, too, sweetheart. I do, too."

They stayed like that for a long moment.

And then Vito had cleared his throat from somewhere behind them, and an umbrella appeared above their heads, casting a gloomier shadow over them.

Her father had looked at his close friend, then back at Gia. "You have family, Giovanna. Lots of family. And you'll always have them. Remember that. You'll always have them."

Gia had tried to find comfort in his words, but she'd only been seven and hadn't really understood what he'd meant in light of losing the closest member of her family. Now she saw what he meant. Now, so many years later, the family had welcomed her back with open arms when she'd decided to return to the fold. Each and every one of them working in unison to help find the person behind her father's death.

Luca included.

She rubbed her arm again, the memory of him sitting across the informal kitchen counter from her a short time earlier replacing the image of her father's rain-stained face.

"Why are you so surprised I came back?" he'd asked her over a simple pasta dinner she'd prepared herself with the help of a jar of homemade pesto sauce the housekeeper/cook had stored in the refrigerator.

Gia had pretended she might not answer the question, even though she'd known she would. "You didn't seem to want anything to do with the family when you left. It just seemed odd that you would come back."

She'd seen something in his blue eyes then. Something that signaled that the still waters of his appearance ran deep within him.

She remembered the many family nicknames for him. The most popular being Pretty Boy Paretti because he had the blond-haired, blue-eyed good looks of the northern Italians rather than the dark intensity of the Sicilians.

It had been those same good looks that made her easy prey when he'd spent a lot of time around the house doing odd jobs for her father while he attended college and then law school. She'd fallen for him, hard.

And the same, she'd thought, had applied to him.

And then his brother was killed and the man she'd fallen in love with had become cold and distant. And then he'd disappeared altogether.

Another movement outside the windows caught her attention. Only the movement hadn't come from outside, had it? Rather she'd caught the reflection of someone moving behind her in the glass.

Gia's heart lodged in her throat as she help-lessly watched a masked man wearing gloves reach above her and then stretch a thin wire cord around her neck.

She moved her right hand up in time to fit it between her neck and the wire before her assai-lant pulled. Still, she coughed from the sudden, intense pressure even as she kicked at his feet and legs. But she was no match for his height and strength. The strong smell of onions filled her nose as he leaned closer to her ear.

"A lady mob boss. You should be glad that you lasted as long as you did, Giovanna. Your father would have been proud."

The voice was unfamiliar to her. Then again, many of the voices that now filled her father's house fell into the same category. Where once she could have foretold someone's arrival by his or her footfalls, now the sound of the house settling kept her up at night.

With good reason, she realized.

She watched her own reflection in the glass. Blood drained from her face and the cord felt dangerously close to severing her fingers as she tried to pull it away, serving only to pull it tighter to the unprotected part of her neck.

Gia kicked out, aiming for the doors, desperately trying to attract the attention of the guard outside. Her bare foot hit a lower pane of glass and the door rattled. She tried again, but found herself jerked out of reach by her assailant.

Death. It had been a way of life for her growing up. Forget that every now and again the house had been the gathering place when someone in the family caught a bullet with his name on it. There were also the more personal deaths. First, there had been the loss of her mother when she was but a girl. And then her paternal grandmother, who had spoken only Italian and had essentially raised her and her brothers until her own death when Gia was seventeen.

But somehow she'd never considered that her own death would take place here. And that it should happen in such a way that she should bear witness to it seemed especially disheartening. She tried to penetrate the mask of the man holding her, catch a glimpse of his eyes, the shape of his jaw, even though the attempt was futile at best. She knew that within a matter of seconds she'd begin to lose consciousness, and soon after that her heart would stop beating due to lack of oxygen.

Still, she searched for a way to fend off her attacker.

It was then she grew aware that when he'd jerked her back from the doors, he'd moved her closer to a side table where a brass lamp sat. She shifted her free hand from around her neck and reached for the light, coughing when he pulled harder on the cord and then reaching again. Her fingertips slid against the cold metal but she couldn't seem to get a grip around the wide base.

The room began to blacken. She slowly blinked, her arm falling to her side.

That was when she caught another reflection in the doors. That of a man coming up behind her attacker.

Luca…

LONG MINUTES LATER, Gia sat against the sofa cushions of the library, her fingers at her raw throat, staring at the man who had appeared out of nowhere and had seen to her attacker with the efficiency of a paramilitary trooper. At least until the last minute when the masked man had landed a punch that set Luca back on his heels and gotten away despite the armed guards who were supposed to be protecting the house and its inhabitants.

Finally, Luca finished talking to the head of the guard detail, who apologized over and over again, and then he closed the library doors, turning to face Gia.

"What are you doing here?"

For the life of her, she couldn't figure out why she was being openly antagonistic toward the man who had just saved her life. Actually, she'd been rude to him pretty much since she'd returned to Long Island. It probably had something to do with the fact that when it came to Luca, it was better to avoid the past than to confront it head-on.

He crossed to a concealed bar, pushed the door to spring it open and poured two glasses of whiskey. He walked toward the couch and handed her one.

He considered her over the rim of his glass as he drank. "I should think your first words to me would be 'thank you.'"

Gia dropped her gaze, the contents of her own glass blazing a trail down her throat. "For all I know, you could have been in on it with him."

His eyes narrowed to dangerous slits. "Is that what you think?"

She shrugged and then put her glass down on the end table nearest her. "It doesn't matter what I think. Facts speak louder than words. And the fact is that I said good-night to you over an hour ago."

Luca stood staring at her for a long moment,

then retrieved something lying on the floor near the door. She realized it was the file of papers he'd had her sign earlier. "I got all the way back to my place before realizing I'd forgotten these."

Gia looked from his hands to his face. "So I should count myself lucky then, shouldn't I?"

He didn't appear to know how to respond so he said nothing. Instead, he moved to sit on the couch next to her.

"Did you get a look at him?" he asked.

"He was wearing a mask."

"That doesn't mean you might not have recognized him."

"I didn't." Her gaze was steady. "Did you recognize him?"

"No," he said easily. "Did he say anything?"

"What was there to say? Beyond 'see you in hell'?"

But he had said something, hadn't he? She put her hand to her temple and rested her elbow against the back of the couch. "Wait. He did say something…" She swallowed hard. "He called me Giovanna and said that I was lucky to have lived as long as I had."

She left out the part about how her father would have been proud. She wasn't sure why. Perhaps it was because she wasn't so sure her father would have been proud. She had not yet avenged his death, she couldn't even keep herself safe.

Besides, he'd never approve of his daughter following in his footsteps. He'd always tried to keep everything involving the family business well away from her. She suspected part of the reason was the sexist double standard to which most men from the old country subscribed. Being a mobster was a man's job. Not a woman's.

Mostly, he probably wanted to protect his only daughter.

She recalled another old-country man with whom she'd had an unnerving visit just that morning. Could Vincenzo Tamburo have been behind the attempt on her life?

"I don't think it's a good idea for you to stay here," Luca said.

Gia looked at him. "Where would you have me go? My place in Manhattan?"

She'd meant the suggestion as a half-assed attempt at a joke. But Luca wasn't laughing. Neither was she, for that matter.

Fact was, he was probably right. She'd known she'd pinned a target to herself when she'd vowed revenge against those responsible for the hit against her father and brother. She'd only thought that so long as she stuck to the house, and stayed away from the windows, she wouldn't be that much at risk.

Mistake number one.

Her gaze dropped to the stern lines of Luca's mouth. And if she wasn't careful, she might give herself over to mistake number two.

A knock at the door and then it opened.

"Miss Gia?"

She sat up a little straighter. "Come in, Vito."

The older Italian entered and stood, taking in the couple on the couch. "I just got word on what happened."

Luca got to his feet to face him. "Aren't you in charge of security, Vito?"

Gia winced. "Luca…"

"No, no, he's right, Miss Gia. I am in charge of security. And there's no excuse for what happened tonight." He looked at the red mark around her neck. "I can only thank God that no more damage was done."

"What did happen tonight?" Luca continued.

Gia sighed, suddenly feeling like she hadn't slept for days. "That's enough, Luca. Thank you…for stopping by." He hiked a brow at her purposeful understatement of his activities. "But I'll be fine now that Vito's here."

Luca looked between her and the old Italian. Then he finally said, "If you're sure."

"It won't happen again," Vito said. "I stake my life on it."

Gia spread her hands palm up as if to say, "See."

Truth was, though, she didn't trust herself where Luca was concerned. In light of all that had happened not just that night, but over the past five weeks, she might be tempted to give in to that soft spot inside her that yearned to curl up in his embrace and take whatever he might have to offer by way of comfort...and sex.

But considering what had happened the last time she'd given herself over to fundamental urges...she looked everywhere but at Luca's questioning gaze.

"Vito will see you out," Gia said.

5

THE FOLLOWING DAY, Luca's words still resonated with Gia. She'd decided to take her morning break in her brother Lorenzo's room and since he was in a deep sleep, she didn't have much else to do than think.

The old bedroom was unusually quiet. The first item on her agenda was to open the heavy curtains so that her brother might see that it was daylight and regain some sense of the passage of time. More than a month's worth that he'd lost and could never regain.

Still, the heavily paneled room felt dark.

Gia let her gaze fall over Lorenzo's face and still form under the blanket. The doctor had been concerned about dehydration so he'd ordered an intravenous feeding tube be inserted a week ago. The stand and bag were on the other side of the bed and was a reminder of why it was so important to pull Lorenzo closer to her rather than let him drift ever nearer to her father and Mario.

Immediately following his emergency surgery to remove two bullets from his lower spine, he'd been placed in a drug-induced coma to allow his body to heal.

The problem was that Lorenzo seemed completely content to remain there, despite her pleas for him to return to some semblance of normalcy.

She needed him.

One of his three full-time nurses came into the room with fresh linens.

"I'm sorry, I didn't know you were in here, Miss Gia." She began backing out.

She gestured for her to come in. "That's okay. I was just about to leave anyway."

The nurse smiled, placed the linens on a rich red oak nightstand and then left the room again.

Gia stared at her brother's impassive face. So handsome. Their father used to like to joke that he didn't look like anyone on the Trainello side of the family and that it was a good thing he was the spitting image of his mother or else he'd have to have him tested to make sure he was of his blood. A broad forehead, smooth dark brows, a slightly hooked nose and strong jawline and tousled glossy dark brown hair that shone almost black against the whiteness of his pillowcase. Growing up, Gia had had her share of friends who had sought out her company in the hopes of a chance to get closer to her older brother.

Which was one of the reasons why the thirty-year-old wasn't married yet. Why should he marry now, he said, when he was enjoying playing a field that widened every time he turned around?

Now he lay alone in a room that was too dark, wallowing in the darkness of his own mind.

She wondered how much of his preference came from not wanting to face the loss of their father and brother. Had she had a choice, she might have gone the same route.

Then again, probably not. Because the time when you had to face the music always came at some point or another. Delaying that moment never helped anything.

A soft rap on the door.

"Miss Gia?"

Frankie. New on the job as her personal assistant and even more tentative with her than he'd been before.

"Come in," she said softly, rising from the chair and bending over to run the back of her knuckles across Lorenzo's warm brow and kiss him on the cheek. "Come back, Lorenzo. I need you."

Frankie opened the door. "I'm sorry to interrupt, but your next appointment is waiting in the office."

"Thank you. I'll be right there."

Long after he left, she exited the room, lingering a moment on the other side of the closed door, examining her options. Then she stepped across the hall to where the nurses were stationed.

"I'm thinking of moving my brother to another room," she said to the nurse who had come in earlier with the linens. "Maybe the change of scenery to someplace brighter will make him want to wake up."

"Yes, ma'am," she said.

Gia frowned as she walked down the hall toward the stairs. She'd never been a ma'am in her life. Even at Bona Dea, she insisted the staff refer to her by her first name, preferring informality over stiffness.

But ever since coming home it seemed everyone was going out of their way to show their "respect" as Frankie had put it. She'd stomached it in the beginning, thinking that her grieving might be part of the reason. But more than a month into her stay, the formality was beginning to chafe.

Lucas was going to stay as close as he could to Gia at all times. Even if that meant enduring her questioning stares when she passed him in the hall. Like now, as she came down the stairs, spotted him and halted as if she'd seen a ghost.

And she was seeing a ghost, wasn't she? Someone who had been a part of her life once, but hadn't been present for a long time. And, apparently, she was having a hard time coming to terms with it.

He let his gaze wander down her sleek body, noting the black mock turtleneck she wore, likely to hide the injury she'd suffered last night at the hands of her would-be killer.

Vito's voice startled him, reminding Luca that the man was there, next to him. "I spoke to Bracco this morning and he says we don't have to worry about that Lancione thing."

Apparently realizing that Lucas wasn't waiting there for her, Gia continued down the stairs into the foyer and then disappeared into the hall that led to the wing of the house that held her father's office. Lucas slid his hand into his pocket and pretended to pace a bit away from Vito who didn't seem to notice his intentions. His new position gave him a clear view into the hallway where three people he recognized rose from their chairs and greeted Gia.

He looked back at Vito. The "Lancione thing" was one way of putting the discovery of Claudio

Lancione's body floating in the East River the week before. The man Gia was rumored to have killed herself.

Lucas straightened his tie. Was she capable of murdering someone? Not just someone, but a man who might be involved in the hit against her father and brother?

He didn't like that he didn't know the answer to the question.

"So homicide detectives haven't been in contact, then?" he asked Vito.

"No. And they won't be. From what I understand from my contact in the department, the authorities are glad to have someone like Lancione off the streets. They see the shooter as having done them a favor."

Not unusual when it came to the NYPD and the mob. The war between the two factions had been going on for so long that both sides had to pick their battles carefully. The death of a lower lieutenant in the Venuto crime family would be viewed as more of a blessing than a curse.

Even though Lucas had suspected that was the way things would go down, he still gave a mental sigh of relief. If Gia had been the trigger woman, she wouldn't have anything to worry about. Which meant that he wouldn't, either.

The outer door behind him opened inward and he and Vito glanced toward the unannounced visitor. Vito had automatically begun reaching for his firearm, more likely in reaction to last night's events than any real concern for a threat.

"Sorry, boss," the guard said as a vaguely familiar young woman who looked as if she'd come straight from a small village in Italy strode into the foyer. Three children under the age of five trailed behind her. Her all black outfit was likely responsible for her rural appearence, and the children wore somber expressions, clad in what Lucas guessed was their Sunday best of slacks and vests. All three were boys, he noted.

"I need to see Miss Gia," the woman said to Vito insistently.

Vito didn't look amused. "I've already explained that Miss Gia is a very busy woman and doesn't have time for a social call."

Then it dawned on Lucas where he had seen her before. At the funeral a month earlier. Her young husband had been Mario's driver and had died along with his employer.

"No social call is this," she said, then continued in Italian.

Lucas easily followed her rapid-fire plea, having been raised as fluent in his parents' native tongue as in English. She was explaining that she couldn't feed her children and needed to appeal for help from Miss Gia.

Vito's expression grew exasperated as he listened. He took something out of his pocket, grasped her hand and put what look like a few hundred-dollar bills into her palm. "There will be no more, DonnaMaria. No more. We're all sorry about your husband, but what happens from here is not the family's concern."

Lucas felt decidedly uncomfortable as he watched the woman's large dark eyes well with tears. He looked down to find two of the children staring at their shiny shoes. The youngest one, however, had honed in on Lucas's curiosity and was openly looking at him.

"This won't pay the rent," DonnaMaria was saying. "Don Vito, please…"

Vito motioned toward the guard still standing inside the door awaiting instructions. "Take her outside," he said.

Lucas opened his mouth to object. To unceremoniously dump the widow and her three children on the doorstep didn't sit well with him. But before he could say anything, Gia came into the hall.

"What's going on?" she asked, taking in the scene before her.

Lucas compared her appearance to the young widow. While Gia was also dressed in all black, there was nothing remotely rural about her. Rather she looked as if she'd stepped straight from the front page of a fashion magazine.

But her clothes were not what impressed him the most. Rather, her sensitivity to what was occurring around her and willingness to get involved did.

The widow glanced at Vito, but being beyond desperate, she advanced on Gia, reaching for her hands and shaking them several times. "Please, please, Miss Gia," she said in Italian.

Vito motioned the guard toward them. "I explained to Mrs. Amato that you're very busy," he said. "Perhaps she can make an appointment for another time."

Gia held her hand up as the guard advanced. "That's all right. I can see her now."

Lucas watched as Gia nodded toward her office. The widow hurried in that direction, the boys shuffling behind. Gia smiled at the children as they marched past her, touching the top of the head of the smallest before following after them.

Lucas listened as the office door closed, leaving the others waiting in the hall. Then Vito let loose a series of Italian curse words.

"Damn woman. She has a business to run. She shouldn't be wasting her time with such mundane details."

How a widow was going to feed her three kids didn't rate as mundane in Lucas's book, but he kept quiet. He, himself, had a much larger agenda to which to attend.

"THANK YOU, thank you, Miss Gia," Mrs. Amato repeated, shaking her hand when Gia rounded the desk to see her out of the office.

The woman raised Gia's right hand as if to kiss it and Gia drew it away, taken aback. She hadn't seen such a display of respect since she'd watched the *Godfather* movies. She'd never even seen anyone do that with her father. She wasn't about to allow that to happen, herself.

"I'm glad we could help you out in your hour of need," Gia said.

The three boys had spread out while Gia had talked to the young widow, and DonnaMaria now hurried around the room to urge them back into formation. Gia pictured the foursome in a jagged hand-to-hand line as they made their way back to the train station.

The door finally closed and she stood staring at it as if it was all that separated her from the world.

She'd been raised to believe that family took care of family. If one of them suffered, they all did.

Then why had Vito wanted to turn the widow away?

Her hand went absently to her neck. She hadn't seen much of herself in the young woman, even though they had to be close to the same age. DonnaMaria had chosen a different route. But now that her husband was gone and she had three boys to raise on her own, she would have to reevaluate what she wanted out of life.

Gia hoped she could help her in that endeavor.

She made a mental note to call Bryan at Bona Dea and tell him to alert personnel that she was sending a seamstress their way in the morning. And the generous check she'd written in the widow's name should be enough to see her through the next couple of months until she got back on her feet.

A brief knock on the door. She immediately tensed, imagining it might be Lucas, whom she'd seen with Vito in the foyer speaking with Vito when she'd come downstairs.

Would there come a time when she wouldn't lose her breath when she looked at him?

"Miss Gia?" Her assistant opened the door.

She relaxed against the front edge of the desk. "Come in, Frankie."

The young man entered, hands laden with a tray of coffee and biscotti. He quickly closed the door after himself with his foot, and Gia lurched forward to take the tray from him before he could splash the liquid on top of the Persian rug. Or, worse, on her.

"Sorry," he mumbled, turning red to the tips of his ears. "I'm not very good at these kinds of things."

"That's all right. I'm a little clumsy with items of a domestic nature myself." She smiled and set the tray on the coffee table.

Actually, Frankie didn't seem good at much of anything. Ask him to bring you a file, and chances were he'd get the wrong one. Answer the phone, he'd butcher the caller's name. Send him on an errand, and he'd call five minutes later, completely lost.

Despite all that, Gia liked him. He was genuinely enthusiastic and she had a feeling he'd offer up his right hand should she ask him to part with it.

Of course, she never would. But just knowing that someone as apparently loyal as Frankie was nearby made her feel better.

Besides, his bumbling made her feel...well, not so out of her element.

Frankie cleared his throat. "I just wanted to tell

you that your ten o'clock is here. And that your eight forty-five, nine o'clock and nine-thirty are still waiting outside."

Gia sighed and rounded her desk. "So many people wanting to meet with me." She sat down and looked over the schedule that Frankie had made out, his handwriting barely legible, but getting better. "I know you didn't work directly for my father, but was his meeting schedule this busy?"

"Oh, yes, Miss Gia. Every Monday and Wednesday the driveway was always full with people wanting to talk to your father."

She nodded, having suspected the same.

Still, it didn't relieve the dread of the day stretched out before her—a day full of people asking for favors, offering to return favors and generally wanting to get in good with what was apparently the new boss of the Venuto family.

Gia stared at her schedule without really seeing it. Is that what she was? When had her hunger for revenge expanded to include family business as usual?

And what did she do when that business as usual deterred her in her hunt to find her father's killer?

Another knock at the door. Without waiting for a response, Luca entered.

The contrast between Frankie and her tall, handsome ex-lover struck her in the gut, reminding her of another reason she might have taken a liking to the thin teen. He wasn't a threat.

"May I have a minute?" Luca asked in a deep baritone that resonated throughout the room.

"I'm sorry, I don't have a minute to give right now. Surely it can wait until another time?" She looked at Frankie. "Send in my next appointment."

"Yes, Miss Gia."

Lucas caught the young man's sleeve as he passed. "Send them in in five minutes."

Frankie looked from Lucas to Gia.

Finally, Gia sighed and nodded.

Frankie hurried through the door and closed it, leaving Gia in a position she didn't want to be in so early in the morning. Or, rather, that she'd prefer not to be in at all.

Alone with Lucas…

6

SECRETS. They could be as deadly as they were dangerous.

And in Lucas's case they were as necessary as the air that he drew into his lungs with every breath.

"Vito believes he might know who made the attempt against your life last night."

Gia could be as hard as nails when she wanted to be. But this information seemed to be the hammer that drove her into the wall. Lucas watched her hand go to her neck as if of its own accord, the fear that flickered through her eyes undeniable.

And his own response was equally powerful.

A protectiveness he hadn't felt in a very long time expanded within him until he was filled with the desire to sweep her into his arms and spirit her away—away from this house, from this family, this dangerous environment—and take her somewhere safe. Somewhere where he could watch over her twenty-four/seven. Somewhere

where he could explore his conflicted emotions for her.

Somewhere where no one could ever hurt again.

The problem lay in that he was positioned as her greatest betrayer.

"It's my guess that it's whoever was responsible for the hit against my father," Gia said, obviously attempting to inject some metal into her voice and falling short of the mark.

"Maybe. Maybe not."

She leaned back in the chair and for a moment Lucas was reminded of her father. Giovanni Trainello had responded in the same way when he wanted answers to oftentimes unanswerable questions.

"I don't think I have to tell you that there's been some dubious response to your taking the helm of the family business, as it were."

"No. No, you don't have to tell me that."

He didn't suppose he did. From what he could tell, she'd already met with each of the other four heads of the rival crime families over the past week. And he didn't think they'd gone all that smoothly. There had even been thinly veiled threats to take over the Venuto family by absorbing it directly into one of the other families. All four of which wanted the honor.

The Venuto family was the most successful of the five major families in New York City. Some attributed it to the fact that Giovanni Trainello had been a smart leader. Others, that he kept a strong army.

But in the past year, Lucas had come to understand that the reason was more complicated than that. Or perhaps simpler. Giovanni Trainello had been a fair man. And as a result, he inspired loyalty in others, commanding a respect that trumped smarts and fear any day of the week.

He squinted at Gia, seeing the same quality in her.

"So are you going to share the information with me? Or do you want me to guess?" she asked.

Lucas smiled, only then realizing that he had yet to continue. "Are you familiar with the name Giglio?"

She went silent for a moment, apparently thinking. "Are you talking about Carlo Giglio? Wasn't he one of Dad's soldiers?"

"His top hit man."

She nodded. "Wasn't he convicted in two of his many killings? Received two life sentences?"

"Yes." He admired her recall ability. "But his attorney just sprung him on a technicality."

Gia's brows rose. "When?"

"Yesterday morning."

Her hand again made its way to her fabric-covered throat.

He didn't like sharing this kind of information with her. Not if it meant watching the unbearable flash of expressions on her beautiful face.

At the same time, he hoped it would give him the leverage he needed to get her to drop her stubborn vendetta and allow him to protect her.

"Has he tried to contact the family yet?"

Smart girl. "No. At least not directly."

"Meaning he hasn't called Vito?"

"Meaning that, yes."

"Who has he been in contact with?"

Lucas considered the chair in front of him but decided to remain standing. "The Guarino brothers."

The color blanched from her face.

Joey and Gino weren't members of rival families. They were long-standing members of the Venuto family, their status coming into question for the first time a week ago when they refused to honor a debt owed to Gia's father. Or, rather, they refused to recognize her as the new, however temporary, head of the family.

"Are you sure?"

"As sure as I can be about anything of this nature. Vito himself shared the news with me just now."

She absently scratched her forehead, considering the information.

Coincidence that an attempt would be made on her life mere hours after one of the Venuto family's head hit men should be given a get-out-of-jail-free card? Lucas didn't think so.

"But he was still in prison when my father was hit."

Lucas nodded. "That he was."

He didn't say anything further because both of them knew that there were plenty of examples of family heads continuing to run their entire operation from behind bars. It wasn't easy. And it required the institution of a whole new language in order to do so, along the lines of "buying a side of beef" meaning hit him now, immediately. "Grill some steaks" meaning burn down someone's business.

"Ask her out on a date" might mean take Gia Trainello out. Permanently.

Gia looked at him point-blank. "Have you ever met Giglio?"

Lucas was surprised by the question. "Actually, I have. I originally represented him in the two murder trials until the case took a nosedive and your father pulled me off in exchange for a closer."

A closer was an attorney renowned for making great closing statements that more times than not convinced the jury to swing his way. An orator, a pleader, a consummate liar.

Little had Giovanni known that Lucas was more than capable in all those departments.

Still, he hadn't argued the reassignment. It hadn't been easy repping a guy he knew was responsible for countless deaths.

"What kind of impression did he make on you?"

Lucas considered her. "Do you mean, did he look like a mass murderer?"

She frowned. "Something like that."

"Surprisingly, no, he didn't. He looked like Uncle Marco down the block. An unassuming type of guy you wouldn't look twice at if you passed him on the street." He shrugged. "One who definitely supports the saying that you can't judge a book by its cover."

"Do you think he's behind the attempt on my life last night?"

Lucas couldn't be sure. But telling Gia that wouldn't further his objective. "Depends on how much stock you put into coincidences."

She nodded.

"Then tell Vito to pull him in."

Lucas inwardly tensed at how casually she issued the order.

Pulling Giglio in didn't mean invite him over for pasta and a chat. It meant literally pulling him by snatching him from his apartment or off the street and tying him to a chair in some remote location. Quite possibly torturing him to find out if he had anything to do with the attempted hit.

Nine times out of ten, it could also mean killing him, or nearly killing him, in order to extract the information.

Gia was watching him curiously, so Lucas said, "Do you want to be present for the meeting?"

He felt relieved at her visible wince. She swiveled in her chair to face the fireplace. "No. No, that won't be necessary."

"And if it's determined that he had something to do with last night's incident?"

She turned to face him fully, the hard-as-nails look back in her eyes.

"Then fire him."

GIA SAT at the kitchen counter, bent over a sheaf of papers concerning the Venuto family holdings, the only sound in the room of her pouring a splash of wine into her glass. She sipped the Chianti, then put the glass down and pinched the top of her nose.

It was after 2:00 a.m. One of Gia's least favorite parts of the day. Gone were the back-to-back meetings and endless phone calls. Gone were the evolving theories on who might ultimately be responsible for her father's death. Gone were the men constantly milling about the place trying to protect her and now going about their own business. Gone was Luca Paretti.

She picked the glass up again, her fingers tightening on the stem, and drained its contents, reaching for the bottle to refill it again.

She wasn't exactly certain when it had happened, but soon after recovering from the shock of having Luca back in her life, in whatever professional manner, she'd begun to notice a desire within her to see him. A knock on her office door? She hoped it was Luca. Step out to stretch her legs? She hoped she'd run into him.

It was enough to drive a woman to distraction. Or to drink.

She got up to discard the empty wine bottle and to open a new one.

She would have liked to blame the change in her long-held feelings for Luca on the precariousness of her current position. Or even on the lack of sleep, which she was definitely suffering from lately. It seemed as if all day she looked forward to these quiets moments to herself. Then when they arrived, she didn't want them, or the fear and loneliness and grief they brought with them.

Any sort of muffled sounds from somewhere inside the house would shoot fear into her veins. And then all the things she hadn't had time to think about during the day crowded in and demanded to be dealt with. She'd come up with an idea or have a question about one of her father's accounts and there was no one around to discuss it with.

"Mind if I join you?"

Gia nearly dropped the bottle she held, so unprepared had she been to hear Luca's voice from behind her.

"My God, scare the crap out of a body already." She moved her free hand over her fluttering heart. Although surprise was mostly to credit for her reaction, she couldn't ignore that his appearance when she'd longed for company—especially his company—was also responsible for her accelerated heart rate.

"What…what are you still doing here?" she asked.

She'd been so certain she was alone in the

house. Okay, perhaps *alone* wasn't the word. Not with Lorenzo upstairs along with his nurses, and the guards out of sight but not out of mind.

"Vito and I had a few things to go over."

Gia crowded the bottle of wine to her chest as she looked at him. "Define 'things'."

"The fact that we can't seem to find Giglio."

He passed her and took a wineglass from a shelf above the counter. He held his hand out for the bottle she still grasped like it was all that stood between her and a charging bull.

"Oh. Sorry." She handed him the bottle.

His blue eyes sparkled at her as he poured himself some wine, and then refilled her glass.

"I was thinking about staying here for a while," he said.

Gia blinked. He'd said the words as casually as if he'd been commenting on the weather.

Normally one might wait to be invited to stay as a guest at someone's house. But even Gia realized that there was nothing normal about her situation...or the man before her who made her even more acutely aware of her loneliness.

"I don't know if that's such a good idea," she said.

He handed her her glass. "Why?"

Should she tell him that sleeping at all was difficult enough without knowing he was under the same roof? Mere doors away from hers? Sleeping between sheets that had come from the house's linen closet? Showering under the same spray provided by a common water source?

Being around every corner as she often found herself hoping throughout the day?

To include nights in that…

"I just don't," she said, passing him. She put her glass on the counter and began gathering the papers she'd been studying.

"Not a good enough reason."

"Yes, well, you're not the one calling the shots here, are you?" She turned to face him. First mistake.

"No. I suppose I'm not."

He stepped imperceptibly closer. Gia's pulse leaped and she was suddenly hot all over.

"Tell me, Gia," he said softly, his gaze dropping to her mouth and then back up again. "What's the real reason you give me the cold shoulder every time our paths cross?"

Gia found herself wetting her lips.

"Is it because you can't stand to be near me?" He reached out and fingered a strand of her hair. "Or could it be that you don't trust yourself when we're alone?"

"There's another option in there somewhere."

"Such as?"

Gia swallowed hard, suddenly wishing the little distance that remained between them would disappear. Not just physically but emotionally.

The truth was, she missed the onetime closeness she'd shared with Luca so many years earlier. Somewhere down the line she'd managed to convince herself that what they had shared had been a summer fling, puppy love, an unrealistic relationship as viewed through the rose-colored glasses only a teenager could get away with wearing. And by doing so, she could dismiss it.

But she'd also come to understand that if you exchanged rose-colored glasses for more practical shades, the world looked gray.

In many instances, she preferred to view it pink.

"Like maybe you no longer have a place in my life," she said.

He put his glass down on the counter next to hers and then pushed both aside. "Oh, I don't know. From where I stand, I think there might be a small place for me to sneak in." He stepped closer still, his warm breath fanning her heated cheeks. "A tiny spot I'm determined to claim."

Gia's throat tightened as he leaned in and pressed his mouth against hers…

7

GIA TASTED like dry red wine and yearning.

The last thing on Lucas's mind when he'd gone to the kitchen to get something to drink had been to seduce the house's current mistress. But when he'd seen her standing there clutching the wine bottle between her full breasts and looking at him like he was just the person she'd wanted to see, he'd been all too ready to react to it.

He was, after all, a mere mortal.

And he doubted few men could have resisted Gia, no matter the mixed signals she gave him whenever he saw her.

Right now, right this minute, she wanted him. And in case he needed further proof of that, she gave it to him. In spades.

The instant his lips touched hers, he felt a spark arc powerfully from her to him. She seemed to sigh against his lips, her body curving into his, her mouth opening not only to give him access to the sweet depths, but also so she could explore the inside of his.

Not in a million years anticipating her response, Lucas's hands encircled her waist. He would have expected her to protest, or perhaps kiss him mildly and then pull away. So he was unprepared for his own reaction to her open and hot answer. The full rush of desire. The need to do everything to her that he'd been wanting since the first moment he'd laid eyes on her again after so long.

No matter that that had been at her father and brother's funeral.

He splayed his hands out above her hips, his thumbs meeting with the bottom swell of her breasts. Her quick intake of breath robbed him of his. He pressed his hips against hers, letting her know of his arousal. And she pushed back, letting him know that she not only understood but that she felt the same.

Sweet Lord in heaven...

Lucas grasped her hips and lifted her to the counter. She was instantly accommodating, pulling him between her thighs and joining her ankles behind him, their kiss growing deeper and more urgent.

Damn, but he had missed her. While he'd had his share of temporary relationships over the years, nothing had compared to what he'd once felt with Gia. What he felt again now. It was as if she'd somehow managed to crawl under his skin, a part of him rather than something separate, setting him aflame with need.

Her fingers went to work on his tie and buttons, slipping her hands inside his shirt when both were only half undone. Her touch was bold and knowing as she pressed her palms against his nipples.

Lucas groaned, shoving his fingers into the back waist of her slacks until he met with the edge of her panties, no comparison to the silk of her skin. He tugged her shirt up and over her head, their mouths barely parting before finding each other again, continuing their kiss even as they shifted to completely remove the summer turtleneck. The instant the fabric whispered to the floor, Lucas honed in on the catch on her slacks, her own fingers fumbling with his belt.

Within moments they were completely nude, Gia's taut nipples poking through the curly hair on his chest, his hands exploring the planes and valleys of her back. He scooped her supple bottom into his hands and pulled her toward the edge of the counter where his erection throbbed. He wanted to lick her all over. He wanted to taste her skin against his tongue. Weigh her breasts in his hands. Explore all the areas he had been longing to explore all week long.

But urgency refused him the leisurely path. He grasped her hips tightly and fit the tip of his engorged arousal just inside her slick wetness, testing her readiness.

She moaned and released her grip around his neck so that she might brace herself against the counter, the bucking of her hips forcing a deeper meeting.

Lucas clenched his teeth tightly and sank into her to the hilt, feeling oddly like it was the other way around and that she was filling him instead. Filling him to overflowing. With need. Pure, hot, unadulterated lust. With an urgency that only she could meet.

Gia arched her back and leaned back farther against her hands, allowing him free view of her magnificent body as he slowly withdrew and then deeply stroked her again. Her breasts swayed, her stomach trembled, every nuance fanning the flames within him more. He wasn't thinking of what he needed to do, or the double life he was leading. He merely lost himself in the moment. In the feel, smell and touch of her.

Releasing his grip on her right hip, he lifted his hand to her breast, curving his fingers under the swollen, fleshy orb. Then he bent to take the tip into his mouth, sucking deeply even as he thrust into her again. One of her hands found its way to the back of his neck where she entangled her fingers into his hair and pulled slightly, the movement not designed to stop him but rather to encourage him.

He switched his attention to her other breast, licking and laving her enlarged nipple until he could feel her trembling through his connection with her.

Lucas then pulled away, withdrawing completely.

Gia blinked her dark eyes open and gasped in protest. He smiled at her, coaxing her to lie back even as he bent toward her stomach, running his tongue from the curve of her breasts down and then back up again, leaving her to wonder where he was heading. Although he didn't need to consult a road map to know exactly where he wanted to go.

He dipped his tongue lower, to the top of her triangle of soft curls. He watched as she closed her eyes and stretched her neck back, as if incapable of bearing another moment of his teasing. Her thighs fell farther open, causing her womanhood to blossom like a pink flower before him, offering up its sweet beauty.

Lucas burrowed his tongue into her curls until he found her magic button, probing it gently, insistently.

Gia called out, climaxing immediately. Lucas held her flat to the counter with a hand on her stomach, relishing the sensation of the spasms kicking against his palm. He ran his tongue along the length of her slit, lapping up her hot juices, aware of the smell of her, the smell of him, on her engorged sex.

Her spasms calmed and he leisurely lapped her clean, no matter how hard his own erection, how fervently he wanted his own release. He moved his attention from her labia to her clit, nipping at the sensitive bit of flesh and earning a surprised cry from her before swirling his tongue around it and gently suckling.

Her rapid breathing told of impending climax. But rather than finishing the job with his mouth, he raised up, hooking the backs of her knees with his arms and pulling her to the edge even as he thrust deeply into her.

"Yes, yes, Luca…please don't stop. Don't ever stop."

His flesh pounded against hers as his thrusts increased in depth and frequency. Sweat covered his brow as he watched her reach her hands across the counter for something with which to brace herself. But there was nothing. And that was the way he wanted it. Because whenever he was around her, he lost his bearings. He no longer knew which way was up or where he was going or what he'd been thinking about the moment before she walked into the room.

And, damn, he wanted…needed her to feel the same. If only for this one moment.

Gia cried out.

Lucas thrust into her twice more and then withdrew, spilling evidence of his own crisis on her thigh instead of inside her.

GIA LAY against the cool counter, feeling oddly exposed beyond her own nudeness, her womb contracting, her breathing out of control. Yet despite all the signs of physical satisfaction, she felt strangely bereft. Disappointed.

It was a sensation she hadn't experienced for a long, long time. In fact, not since the last time she and Luca had had sex.

The realization was jarring.

And no less humiliating.

"Well," she said quietly as he stepped back away from her and began putting on his pants. "Seems like some things never change."

She'd forgotten about his penchant for withdrawing right before he reached orgasm. She'd been on the Pill at the time and had told him that, but still he'd withdrawn, spilling his seed over her stomach rather than inside her.

It had left her feeling betrayed and hurt.

And she felt no differently now. Especially since the method, or any contraceptive method, wasn't one hundred percent effective.

Luca looked at her, as if not understanding the sarcasm behind her words.

Gia didn't care if he understood or not. She scooted from the counter and picked up her own clothes, jerking on her turtleneck first because it would give her the greatest amount of coverage.

Her rational side pointed out that it was a good thing he'd withdrawn. Because now she wasn't on oral or other contraceptives and honestly hadn't even considered the risk of pregnancy when things began getting hot and heavy between them.

But her heart wouldn't hear it.

Because she knew that the last thing he wanted was her to be pregnant with his child.

Luca finished dressing and went to the refrigerator. "How about I make us some eggs?"

Gia pulled on her slacks and put her shoes back on. "How about you find the front door?"

He turned and stared at her, as if unaware he still held the refrigerator door open.

She struggled to do up the fastener on her pants. "Don't look at me that way."

"What way?"

"Like you don't have a clue what just happened."

He blinked at the refrigerator door and closed it before stepping closer to her.

Gia held her hand up to ward him off. "Don't even think about it. I've been stupid enough for one night."

For one lifetime, it seemed, when it came to Luca Paretti.

Emotions roiled within her. Feelings she didn't know what to do with. Sadness, fear…the rekindling of a love long lost.

The knowledge that tonight she had tried to claw at that same love, to try to recapture how it had once felt to love Luca and have him love her, made her stomach drop to her feet.

"Gia…"

"No, please. Don't," she whispered, suddenly aware that her cheeks were damp.

She picked up the papers from the counter and left the room—and Luca—behind.

"I'D RECOMMEND immediate action on this, Gia. The sooner the better."

Gia sat across from her uncle Vito on the couch in her father's office, the morning sun slanting in through the French windows oddly cheerful in light of what he'd just shared with her.

She faced him more fully. Ever since having had sex with Luca on the kitchen counter two nights ago, she'd had trouble concentrating on anything other than where he might be in the house and what he might be doing. A part of her wanted to track him down and order him out.

Another, more traitorous part of her wanted to have sex with him again and force him to climax while inside of her, damn the consequences.

And now Vito was telling her that there were some risky decisions to be made and that she needed to make them.

"How's Lorenzo?" he asked when she didn't immediately respond.

Her hand froze. He knew how her brother was. The nurses told her that Vito went up to visit him twice a day. While it was reported that he was responding more in his new environs—she'd had them put him in their mother's sun-filled old bedroom that was still decorated in pink and white—it wasn't a happy response. He wanted to be moved back to his room.

But since he had yet to start therapy, his spinal injury guaranteed that he couldn't make the move on his own.

And Gia refused to have him moved again.

Damn it, if she had to force him to wake up, so be it. Neither one of them might like it, but she strongly believed it was for the best. She refused to stand back and watch him destroy himself anymore. Beyond the fact that he'd refused to start therapy and thus risked more surgery as his muscles atrophied, he'd lost a great deal of weight, barely taking in more than the drugs the doctor prescribed along with the water required to swallow them.

She had an appointment to meet with the doctor that afternoon to discuss her brother's medications. Her next step was to do away with them all. At this point she knew he was addicted and was dreading seeing him go though withdrawal on top of everything else.

"I have some ideas that I hope will get him moving," she said carefully.

While family was family, she found she didn't like discussing her brother's condition with anyone, save his nurses and doctor. She wanted to protect him until she could figure out what to do. He was the only family she had left.

"Look, Vito, do what you think is best in regards to Joey and Gino Guarino. I trust you implicitly."

"Good. I've made an appointment for you to meet with them both this morning."

8

LUCAS IDLY WATCHED the scheduled morning sweep for listening devices go through the mansion. Slightly agitated, he raked his fingers through his hair and turned his attention to the closed door to Gia's office. Vito had gone in a little while ago and he had yet to see Gia. He assumed she was already inside.

Hell, he didn't have a clue why she'd gone cold on him after their kitchen encounter. He'd lain awake all that night thinking about it. She'd reached orgasm, of that he was sure.

Then why the cold shoulder directly afterward? Morning-after regret?

But no. It appeared that something he'd done or said had been responsible for her change in behavior. But, God help him, he couldn't figure out what it was.

Or why it was bothering him so much.

Mentally considering the list of items he hoped

to discuss with Gia and Vito this morning, he went into the kitchen, greeted the cook, then poured himself a cup of coffee at the counter. The same counter that Gia had been magnificently spilled over two nights ago. Like a glorious meal begging to be eaten.

Damn it all, but his intentions that night hadn't been only to fulfill some sort of short-lived physical need. And sure, he'd accomplished that, but he'd also hoped that by coaxing Gia to let down her guard, she'd also open back up to him emotionally.

He grimaced, recognizing the egomaniacal slant to his thoughts. What was he? Some sort of sex God that turned mere mortal women into lifelong slaves after one night together?

What had made him think that sex—great, mind-blowing sex—would change anything?

If anything, their brief fling had made things even worse.

"Oh, good morning, Mr. Paretti. I didn't see you there."

Lucas glanced up from a summons that had been served a half an hour ago to look at Frankie. He smiled at the kid. In so many ways he reminded him of his younger brother, Angelo. Almost painfully so. Beyond the same lanky physical similarities, the kid displayed the same obsessive desire to be included in the family.

An obsession that had been deadly for his brother.

"How's it going, Frankie?" he said.

"It's going great."

Lucas nodded. "Miss Gia seems to have taken a liking to you."

"Yeah," the eighteen-year-old said with a grin. "Go figure."

Lucas chuckled softly, reminding himself that just because things had turned out badly for Angelo, it didn't mean that Frankie was doomed to the same fate. Especially since he had skipped a few steps and was working directly for Gia now. One might argue that the closer he was to her, the more dangerous the situation. But not with Lucas involved. Right now the only safe spot on the entire estate was near Gia.

"What's on tap for this morning?" he asked.

"I don't know yet. I'm still waiting to go in. But I think she'll probably send me into the city to pick up some sort of design book from Bona Dea. Her partner's been calling every five minutes."

Lucas had all but forgotten about Gia's fashion business. Easy to do, seeing as she seemed to be concentrating more on family business than on design. But he'd come across an idle sketch or two mixed in with official papers, or sometimes scribbled in the margins of draft documents. So apparently she wasn't as strictly focused on family issues as he thought.

The idea that there would come a time when she might leave Long Island for good and return to her normal life in Manhattan left him feeling empty.

Then again, it was said that once in the mob, always in the mob. Would it even be possible at this point for her to ever fully leave Long Island and the Venuto family?

And him? What happened when he achieved his own clandestine objectives? Since it would be impossible for him to conceal his identity once those he fingered on behalf of the FBI were brought to trial, he would never be free to roam any street in New York again. Including Manhattan, where Gia might hope to return to.

Lucas looked at his watch. Vito had been in Gia's office for a while then. He knew Frankie was up bright and early to get his assignments for the day. And if he hadn't spoken to Gia yet, that meant nobody but Vito had.

"Well, okay, I have a couple of things to do

before I go in to see Miss Gia. Have a nice day, Mr. Paretti," Frankie said, waving.

"You, too, Frankie."

He watched the kid leave the kitchen, taking in his gangly form, his loose-limbed gait. A sharp pang hit him in the side. The similarities to Angelo were so great that for a moment it was difficult to breathe.

He heard voices in the hall. He got up and headed in their direction, reaching the foyer just in time to watch Gia kiss Vito's cheeks before the older man turned in the opposite direction and departed.

Gia caught Lucas's gaze and froze, as if unsure how to react. Then she averted her eyes and went back inside her office, closing the door behind her.

Lucas glanced over his shoulder to make sure no one else wanted her immediate attention and then crossed to stand in front of the closed door. He knocked once and then let himself in.

GIA HAD KNOWN Luca would follow her. And, she reluctantly admitted, she'd hoped he would.

She turned to face him, just as he stepped inside and closed the door behind him.

"Good morning," he said quietly.

"What's so good about it?"

Gia rounded her father's desk and sat down heavily.

"Vito had bad news?"

"You tell me. You two seem to talk more than I do."

"I haven't a clue."

She sighed and sat back in the chair. "I'm meeting with the Guarino brothers this morning."

Luca's brows rose slightly on his handsome forehead. "I thought Vito was handling all that."

"So did I."

Gia was surprised that she could discuss items of a professional nature with him so easily, when personally she didn't know whether she wanted to allow herself to love him, or clutch desperately on to the indifference she'd cultivated over the years.

"It seems that Joey and Gino are insistent upon a meeting with me," she said. "And Vito didn't think it was a good idea to refuse the meet."

Lucas nodded as he took the visitor's chair opposite her. "Do you know what you're going to say to them?"

"Oh, I don't know… I was thinking about something along the lines of, 'either pay up or I'll have someone break your kneecaps.' But more original."

"Why fix something that isn't broken?"

She found herself smiling at him despite the

black shadow that eclipsed her heart whenever she thought about what happened in the kitchen.

"Yeah, well, I think it's better if I just play this one by ear without making any physical threats." She fingered the letter opener she'd left out earlier, noting its sharp edges before putting it back in the drawer. "I was hoping to avoid just such confrontations during my brief stint."

"But you've met with Tamburo and the other rival family heads. You didn't avoid them."

"Ah, but that was different. To them, I'm still Daddy's little girl. Mostly they offered their condolences and talked about who was going to take over Dad's interests. I thanked them for their concern and told them I'd think it over."

Gia bit briefly on her bottom lip, reluctant to share the true emotion she'd seen displayed in the others' faces. Especially Tamburo's. When she'd finally dropped off to sleep last night, she'd dreamed of being covered in wet cement. Cement that was being used to create the sidewalk to one of the Venuto family's construction projects in Long Island City. A modern apartment building overlooking the East River with remarkable views of Manhattan to the west.

Of course, if her dream came true, she wouldn't be able to enjoy the view. She'd be dead.

She also knew that the coy feminine responses she had managed to make to Tamburo and the other heads would only buy her a limited amount of time. Before too long she expected them to start making bolder moves toward securing the Venuto family as their own. She absently fingered the fading bruises on her neck. If they hadn't already.

But so long as she had power, she intended to use it to find her father's killers.

And prayed that Lorenzo would snap out of it and take over before she got into any more trouble than she already had.

"Would you like me to be present for the meeting with the Guarino brothers?" Luca asked.

Gia blinked at him. Only a couple of days before, he might have phrased the question differently. Something along the lines of, "I want to be present during the meeting." To which she would have refused him outright.

But his quiet request now made her consider him more thoughtfully.

"Yes. Yes, I'd like that. Thanks."

She met his eyes, seeing something in the deep blue depths that made her remember the better parts of the other night. Her heart contracted in her chest.

Another rapid knock on the door had barely sounded before it flung inward to reveal Frankie, who was out of breath and grinning. "Good morning, Miss Gia," he said exuberantly.

Gia beamed at him, the boy's enthusiasm brightening her dark morning. "Good morning, Frankie. How are you today?"

He looked from her to Lucas. "Should I come back?"

Gia got up and rounded the desk, leaning against the edge with her arms crossed over her chest. "No, that's all right. Lucas was just leaving."

He rose to his feet, towering over her. She was close enough to smell his citrus aftershave. It made her mouth water with the desire to kiss him.

"I'll see you at ten for the meeting, then," she said to him.

He nodded, moving toward the door, where he grasped Frankie's shoulder for a brief squeeze. "Don't work too hard, kid. And try to stay out of trouble."

"I will, Mr. Paretti."

The almost parental affection Luca displayed made Gia's heart ache even further as she watched him close the door.

GIA COULDN'T REMEMBER a time when she'd felt so uncomfortable. Joey and Gino weren't only rude, they were outright confrontational. She hadn't prepared herself for that.

While she knew that they were refusing to honor their debt to her father, she'd expected them to offer up an apology and try to make excuses as to why they weren't paying.

Instead, Joey looked at her point-blank from across the office table and said, "We ain't going to pay."

It was a challenge. She knew that. A challenge to her as temporary head of the family.

A challenge to the integrity of the family.

"We don't mean no disrespect, Gia," Gino said, shrugging his meaty shoulders. "But we don't see how we still owe your father, you know, with his being dead and all."

This was the first time she'd encountered anyone who had disrespected her and her father in the same sentence.

She stared down the man opposite her. Both he and Joey had been around for as long as she could remember. They'd been present at holiday dinners, baptisms, birthday parties and family barbecues. And they'd always looked the way they looked now, bearing a few unwanted pounds, their features droopy and fleshy, their suits having come from a secondhand store and probably worn for the past thirty years.

When she'd welcomed them into her home a little while before, she'd given them kisses on both cheeks and referred to them as "uncle."

Not anymore.

"Don't mean no disrespect?" Vito asked, incredulous. He'd surprised Gia when he'd shown up at the last minute to sit in on the meeting. "What do you call what you just said?"

Luca smoothed down his tie. "Vito's right, Gino. By refusing to pay on this considerable debt, you're showing blatant disrespect to both Miss Gia and the entire Venuto family."

Gia added, "This is money you borrowed from the family. It's money you owe. It's a simple as that. Pay it."

Gino sat back and looked a breath away from spitting over his shoulder. "There ain't no Venuto family anymore. That died along with your father and brother."

"Not so long as I'm on this side of the ground," Vito said, nearly catapulting from his chair.

Both Gia and Luca grasped the older man before he could put his hands around Gino's neck.

Both Gino and Joey rose from their chairs,

picked up their hats and began backing toward the door.

"Yes," Gia said. "Perhaps it would be best if you both left now. Took some time to think about what you've just said. Reconsider your position."

She released Vito when she was sure Luca had him under control. She rounded the table and stood over the two men, crossing her arms. She towered over them by at least five inches.

Joey put on his hat, openly scowling at her. Gino looked a little more sheepish, holding his hat against his chest. "You gotta know, I had the utmost respect for your father, Gia—"

"That's 'Miss Gia' to you," Vito spat out.

Joey looked at him and back at Gia. He shrugged. "Sorry. But word's out that there ain't no Venuto family no more. And Gino and me...well, we gotta look out after our own interests, if you know what I mean."

Gia stared at him for a long moment, and then she smiled. Mostly to cover for her clenched teeth. "I understand, Joey. I understand."

She took him by the arm and led him toward the door, Gino following after them. She kissed them both on the cheeks. "Thanks for letting me know where you stand."

The two men looked at each other, then walked

into the hall, expressions of triumph visible on their faces.

Gia closed the door, waited a moment, and then looked at Vito.

"Torch their restaurant."

9

MUCH LATER that night, Lucas closed the door of the Queens safe apartment behind him, the complicated happenings of the day forefront in his tired mind. He'd had to wait to leave the estate until he was sure Gia was settled in for the night, but needed to get out of there before any permanent damage was done to the Guarino brothers' restaurant.

Then again, there might be little he could do. He'd found out pretty quickly a year ago that the FBI wasn't interested in small fish. They wanted the big ones. They wanted to bring the entire New York City syndicate down, no matter how far-reaching and improbable that goal was. He'd only been on the job for a week and had stumbled across information on a bank-truck heist. He'd fully expected the FBI to intervene. Instead, the robbery was allowed to go ahead as scheduled and one of the truck's guards had taken a bullet that had paralyzed him for life.

When he'd talked to his handler later that night, he'd been furious. His handler had merely told him to get over his inexperience and accept that an interception would have revealed that the burden had a source planted within the family. And that it would be only a matter of time before they figured out it was Lucas.

He'd suffered innumerable incidents since, many of them inspiring him to wonder if he was making any impact at all against the crime family. If they were allowed to go ahead with the violent side of their business as usual, what was he accomplishing?

Of course, he eventually came back to the understanding that his satisfaction would come in the end. That while his actions didn't stop the dozen or so incidents in the past year, they would end any future episodes.

Although, every now and again he pondered whether that would even be the case. Because it seemed that for every criminal that was knocked out of the ring, another five popped up to take their place.

The thought brought the memory of Gia's beautifully determined face to mind.

"Torch their restaurant."

The restaurant, of course, referred to Joey and

Gino Guarino's Italian eatery in Brooklyn. And that within the blink of an eye Gia had gone from successfully talented fashion designer to ruthless mob boss.

It didn't really matter that she'd qualified her order, requesting that only a small kitchen fire be set—one that would only do enough damage to get her point across. The fact that she was already resorting to violence to solve family problems indicated that she'd crossed from the tentative shadows into broad daylight. And that he would have a harder time protecting her. Not only from rival families. But from the FBI and himself.

What role she might or might not have played in Claudio Lancione's death could be written off as a crime of passion.

What she was involving herself in now was willful criminal conduct.

One of the Quantico criminal psychologists had spoken to his freshman class on the thin line between right and wrong and how easy it was to mentally justify crossing it.

"If your family is hungry and you pass a casserole cooling on a windowsill of a house, you may think yourself justified in taking it. But what if you learned that the family you had stolen from hadn't eaten a decent meal in over a week, either, and that they'd just scraped up enough money to buy the ingredients necessary to make that casserole?" He'd held up a finger. "One minor detail changes the whole schematic. And it's those details you'll have to master in your role as an agent, because they're what make all the difference."

The cell phone finally rang.

He picked up on the second ring.

"What delayed you?" his handler asked.

"A lot of activity at the house."

"Do you have it on tape?"

"Yes."

"Take them to the usual drop-off point."

After arranging a time for their next exchange, the phone call ended. Lucas hadn't even had a chance to consider whether he should have mentioned the order for a fire at the Guarinos'. He frowned.

Rising, he shrugged into the track jacket that made him look a little shorter, a little wider, and then picked up the box with the tapes—tapes that didn't include Gia or her orders—feeling a bit like the man who'd just stolen the casserole from the windowsill.

GIA SAT next to Lorenzo's bed in her mother's old room, a single lamp throwing a warm pool of light onto the off-white area rug covered in tightly knit rosebuds. When her mother was still alive, Gia used to like to come in here and watch her get ready for a night out with her father. She'd lie across the canopy bed, chin propped on her hands, and gaze lovingly at a mother as beautiful outside as she had been inside.

But it was the memory of her father's words that haunted her.

"Trust no one, Lorenzo. No one. Even family will betray you under the right circumstances."

Gia looked from the rug to her brother's sleeping face. She recalled the scene as clearly as if it had taken place yesterday instead of nearly twenty years ago. Her mother had finished with dinner, and Gia had been asked to call her father and brothers to the dining room. Of course, calling meant going to get them, not actually shouting for them to come.

But when she'd found the door to her father's office ajar, and heard his voice, she'd hesitated from barging right in and instead had stood outside and peeked around the frame.

Giovanni Trainello had been standing over a twelve-year-old Lorenzo, one hand on the boy's skinny shoulder while he shook his index finger between them.

"Do you hear me? Trust no one."

"Okay, Father. I won't."

"You can only rely on yourself in this world. The rest…well, the rest will do its damn best to surprise you at every turn."

Lorenzo had always been anxious to please their father. Coming when he was called. Enduring adult directives like the ones he'd received that night.

The words were in sharp contrast to what Gia had been used to hearing, and while she hadn't completely grasped the importance of them, they had remained with her, always. If only because of the somber, serious tone her father had used when normally he was a jovial, happy man. At least when it came to his wife and three children.

Now she wondered if he'd ever had a meeting similar to the one she'd experienced today. And pondered if that was the reason she remembered that exchange between father and son so long ago.

She glanced at her watch, feeling a pang of regret that she'd had to give the order she had. The Guarino brothers had worked so very hard to make their restaurant into a place where everyone in the family was welcome. They'd opened it forty years ago and it had always been a Brooklyn mainstay. It hurt to have to order that a part of it be destroyed, even if it was just a small part.

But the only alternative was to have Joey and Gino roughed up. And seeing as both of them were in their sixties, she didn't think that was such a good idea. Her moral code wouldn't allow her to do anything of that nature.

Then again, the unspoken threat that they'd lose the restaurant altogether if they didn't pay up would probably hurt the brothers more than a leg fracture. It would probably break their very hearts.

She closed the design book she had open on her lap and stood, stretching the kinks out of her neck before kissing Lorenzo on the cheek and then shutting off the light.

She let herself out into the hall, turned toward her room, and ran straight into Luca.

DAMN. Lucas had done everything in his power to make sure he didn't bump into anyone on his way back into the house. Especially not Gia.

Which amused him not at all, because he usually went out of his way to make sure he did see her.

"Oh!" she said, clearly surprised by bumping into him.

He caught her arms before she either toppled over or dropped the book she held.

"I was just calling it a night," he said.

She blinked at him, her beautiful features in shadow. "I was just sitting with Lorenzo before going to my room."

He looked toward the closed door. "Any change?"

She dropped her gaze to the floor and shook her head.

Lucas tried to make it up to see Lorenzo at least once a day. He had yet to have a meaningful conversation with the eldest Trainello brother since the hit. No one had. Even the NYPD detectives working the case wanted access to him so that they could piece together what had gone down that night. Seeing as he was the only survivor, he was the only one who might give any of them any clue.

He looked at Gia more closely. Of course, she had other reasons for wanting her brother to recover.

"Were you out?" she asked. "You smell of fresh air."

Lucas grimaced. "Yes. I went outside for a cigarette."

He didn't like lying to her. Particularly since

she was one of the few people he had never been very good at lying to.

Present circumstances aside.

Although he suspected that if she came straight out and asked him if he was working undercover for the bureau, he would tell her the truth.

"I don't smell smoke."

He smiled even though inside he berated himself for his stupid mistake. He couldn't afford to arouse any suspicion now. Not when he was afraid things were about to get very dangerous, very quickly. "I decided against it once I got outside," he told her. He took the pack of cigarettes from his pocket. "You want one?"

She laughed quietly. "You don't know how good that sounds right now."

He put the pack away. "Rough night?"

"Rough month." She sighed and hugged the book she held to her chest.

He nodded. "It couldn't have been easy to make that call this morning."

"No. No, it wasn't. That restaurant is the brothers' life."

"I know. But the order had to be made."

"I suppose. It's just that…"

Lucas waited, taking the opportunity to appreciate her pretty face. Hoping against hope that he hadn't lost her yet.

"I wish things could have worked out differently."

"Yes," he said. "I do, too."

He discovered that he was touching her, his hand on her right arm. He caressed her skin left bare by her silky black tank top.

He took his hand back. "Look, Gia, about the other night…"

She blinked up at him.

"If I did or said anything to upset you, I'm sorry."

Gia looked everywhere but at him. He hoped that she'd tell him what he'd done. What he'd said.

But she remained quiet. Perhaps rethinking the situation herself.

"You know," she said finally, "there was a time when I thought the sun rose and set on you. That I couldn't imagine taking a breath without smelling you. Couldn't imagine living without you walking beside me." Her chin was tucked into her chest as she said the words. But she looked up at him now, the dampness in her eyes making them appear luminescent. "I can't do that again, Luca. I can't."

She shook her head as if trying to control her emotions.

"I see you and I'm torn between wanting to run flat out in the other direction and holding on to you so tightly that you can't get away again." She laughed softly without humor. "When it comes to you, it's all about extremes. Either or. In or out. There is no middle ground. No compromise. And, frankly, that scares the hell out of me."

Lucas threaded his fingers through the hair over her right ear and pulled her close, cradling her head against his chest. "I know. Trust me, I know."

A sense of powerlessness burst within him, but so did a command so all consuming that he was nearly knocked back on his heels by the strength of it.

Or was Gia, herself, responsible for that?

"You can't possibly know," she whispered, flattening her hand against his chest, though she didn't try to move away.

Lucas reached down and tipped her chin up with his free hand. "Yes, I can," he murmured, allowing his gaze to roam over her beautiful face. "I know because I feel the same."

10

TIME AND DISTANCE should have erased the memory of Luca's gentle touch and quietly spoken words from the night before, but as Gia stared out the conference-room window of Bona Dea's Manhattan offices, not really seeing the city's soaring, jagged skyline, she imagined that she could feel the warmth of his touch even now. As if somehow the tender contact had branded her more lastingly than any flesh-melding grasp made in the throes of passion.

She turned back toward the conference table where Bryan and the rest of the staff animatedly discussed the final details of the coming showing of the company's spring collection. The heated debate had turned to the selection of the ensemble that would appear as the centerpiece of the show.

But somehow what had once been the reality of her life emerged surreal. She sensed that she could as easily have been dreaming the scene before her as living it.

"Gia?" Bryan asked.

She realized the room had gone quiet and that most likely a question had been asked of her. A question she hadn't heard.

She lightly shook her head and smiled. "I'm sorry. I was just thinking about how I don't like this color much. It's so retro early 90s."

She crossed the room to the three models standing there and adjusted the sash on the raincoat-like shirtdress the one on the right wore.

The table erupted into "I told you so's" and objections, just as Gia predicted it would.

In all honesty, she really didn't care about the color or its relationship to a prior fashion year. She'd been looking to divert attention from her distractedness, and she'd succeeded.

Her new position in the room allowed her a view outside the glass window separating the conference room from the rest of the Bona Dea offices. The sight of the armed gunman that had escorted her inside, watching passersby, made her shiver.

"I think we've accomplished all that we're going to accomplish this a.m.," Bryan said, rising from the table.

Everyone agreed, and after a few moments, the room was empty but for Bryan and Gia.

She turned to face him. "I guess I was as helpful here as I am from Long Island."

Bryan didn't say anything. He merely gathered his papers together on the conference table.

Gia moved to stand next to him, laying her hand on his sleeve. "I'm sorry, Bry. I truly am. I...when I decided to look after my father's estate, I never planned that I'd be there this long."

He straightened from his slightly hunched posture and looked directly at her. "Didn't you?"

She didn't know what to say, so she said nothing.

He sighed heavily. "That was uncalled for. It's just that I was afraid something like this was going to happen when you went out there." He looked at her beseechingly. "I need you here, Gia. This is a make-or-break time for us. And I can't do it on my own."

She raised her hand to touch his handsome cheek. "I beg to differ. From what I can see, you're doing a bang-up job of it by yourself."

"That's because you don't see what's going on behind the scenes. Designer rebellions, lost pieces, sick models..."

"Sounds like a normal day at work to me."

He chuckled quietly. "Yes. Maybe you're right. But we both agreed when we partnered up that we were doing it because neither one of us thought we could toe the line on our own."

"Agreed. But that was five years ago."

"What difference does that make?"

"Five years' worth of difference."

He turned his attention back to putting sketches into his case. "Is there something you're trying to tell me here, Gia?"

Was there?

Gia had certainly not come there this morning with any sort of agenda. Bryan had asked her to come, and she had.

But now she realized that the best thing she could do for Bryan, for herself, was admit that it wasn't fair to either one of them to pretend she could handle both her duties at Bona Dea and the Venuto family without jeopardizing one or the other. And while pulling out of the company she had built up with Bryan from scratch would put incredible stress on him, to not do so wouldn't be right, either.

He finished what he was doing and looked at her again, waiting for an answer.

She merely smiled at him sadly.

Bryan groaned and hugged her.

"Oh, sweetie, I'm so sorry if I sound like the biggest of all bitches. It's just that I miss you around here."

"I know. I miss you, too," she murmured.

He nodded as he pulled back. "I think I believe you."

"Why wouldn't you?"

He shrugged. "I don't know. It looks like the title Lady Boss might fit you a little too well." He looked over her all-black ensemble. "I didn't want to say this, Gia, but you've changed."

She swallowed hard. "But you still love me, right?"

His grin was automatic and all encompassing. "I'll always love you, dear. You're the only woman who ever made me wonder what it might be like to swing the other way."

Gia laughed and hugged him again, thinking of all the struggles they'd had over the past five years, all the triumphs. From working out of a musty old warehouse downtown, to opening their first boutique on Fifth Avenue, they'd been through a lot together.

But she had the cheerless sensation that this was where their road together ended and where they would now have to continue on alone.

An image of Luca slid through her mind and

she clutched Bryan even closer. If only she could ask her friend's advice about the mysterious man who had invaded her heart once again.

But to talk about it would only make it that much more real.

Bryan seemed to catch sight of something over her shoulder. "God, can't you make those guys dress any better? They look like gravediggers."

Gia glanced toward the door where the one gunman had been joined by another. The first one opened the door without knocking.

"Miss Gia, your presence is required at the estate."

She looked at Bryan, who raised a brow at the stilted speech. "Your presence is required at the estate," he repeated.

She kissed him soundly. "So it would seem."

She started to turn from him and then hesitated.

He waved her away. "Go on. I'll be fine. Bitchy as all hell, but fine." He crossed his arms over his chest. "Now go before a gunfight or something breaks out and blood gets all over our spring line."

GIA HAD CERTAINLY been in taxis before, and even rented a limo every now and again for fashion events, but she wasn't used to being driven everywhere she went. While it did give her more time to get work done in the New York stop-and-go traffic, she didn't feel comfortable knowing that the driver heard every word she spoke on her cell phone, and knew exactly where she went and why.

She understood it was for safety's sake, but the practice still bothered her.

Yet when they finally pulled through her father's gated driveway entrance to find three NYPD cruisers parked at odd angles in front of the house, and two unmarked vehicles parked before them, she wanted to ask the driver how good he was at car chases, because she wanted to go everywhere but inside.

"What's going on?" she asked the driver.

"Sorry, Miss Gia, but I couldn't say."

Couldn't say or wouldn't say, Gia found it didn't matter. She'd find out soon enough.

The car came to a halt and she climbed out of the back.

"Miss Trainello, I was wondering if I might have a moment," a man in a suit asked, coming to stand in front of her.

"And you might be?"

"Detective Sudowski."

"In which division?"

"Homicide."

The ground slanted under Gia's feet.

"On the advice of her attorney, Miss Trainello has nothing to say."

Gia heard Luca's voice before she saw him. And she'd never been so relieved to see anyone in her life.

He circled the detective, staring at her meaningfully and offering his arm for her to take. He began to lead her to the front doors of the house.

"Miss Trainello, Miss Trainello!" a reporter she recognized from the funeral called out. "What do you have to say about Joseph Guarino's death and the suspected arson that killed him?"

"Oh, God," Gia whispered.

Luca's arm went around her waist, half supporting her, half pressing her onward into the house.

LUCA STOOD BACK, watching the chaos unfold around him. Gia's office was filled with people offering up differing opinions on what had happened. The only silent ones were Gia and him.

Gia, herself, sat behind the desk looking like someone had poisoned her breakfast. Her already pale skin was ten shades whiter and she absently rubbed her stomach as if afraid she might throw up.

"All right, I think it's time for everyone to leave and let Miss Gia consider everything that's been said."

She looked at him at first in surprise, then in gratitude. Then she stood. "Everyone but Vito."

The older man nodded and sat back down.

Within moments, the room emptied out, leaving just the three of them. Lucas closed the door.

Gia rounded the desk and leaned against it, gripping the edges as if the wood was the only thing keeping her steady. "What happened, Vito?"

The older man shrugged. "I don't know, Gia. My men said the place was empty before they torched it. Joey must have found a way inside without them seeing him between the time they checked and the wick was lit, so to speak."

Lucas stepped forward. "The fire was supposed to be contained in the kitchen."

"Jesus." Gia crossed her right arm under her breasts and rubbed her brow with her other hand. "How could this have happened? I wanted them warned. I didn't want one of them killed."

The room went silent.

Vito cleared his throat. "While Joey's death certainly wasn't planned, it may end by working out better in the long run."

Gia and Lucas stared at him.

He shrugged again. "The other debtors who've refused to pay you what your father was owed will think twice before refusing again."

"We're talking about a man's death, Vito."

"As luck would have it, I've already heard from Gino Guarino. Our guys are picking up the full amount due from him this morning."

Gia closed her eyes as if concentrating on keeping her breakfast down.

Lucas stepped forward. "The hows and whys aren't what's important now, Gia. What is important is that you have half the NYPD parked in your driveway and every five minutes another television crew arrives."

She looked at him as if wishing him to make it all go away. And, for the life of him, he wanted to make it happen.

"What do you think I should do?" she asked.

"I'd suggest making a statement to the media. Something along the lines of you and your family mourn the loss of a close friend and send your condolences to his family."

Vito grunted. "Your father wouldn't have done any such thing."

"What would he have done?" Gia asked him.

"He would have had his men chase the media

off and stonewalled the cops until they went away."

She looked at Lucas.

He grimaced. "It could work."

She rounded the desk and took a pad from the middle drawer. "I'm going to make a statement and offer to speak to the police."

Lucas nodded.

"What in the hell will you say?" Vito demanded.

"That from all we know, Joey's death was a terrible accident, and beyond that we know nothing."

11

THAT AFTERNOON, after Gia had addressed the media and had spoken briefly to the police, Lucas stood near the front windows considering the empty driveway, when his cell phone rang. He pulled it out of his inside jacket pocket and looked at it. "Unknown Caller," the display read.

He looked over his shoulder to make sure no one could hear him.

"Hello," he said normally.

"I need to talk to you. As soon as possible," his FBI handler said.

Lucas disconnected and put the phone back in his pocket.

Damn. He didn't want to leave Gia alone. Not now when she finally appeared to be depending on him, in however limited a capacity.

But to ignore his handler's request would be akin to breaking his own cover. The next step in the communication process would be to send someone in undercover, either as a package or pizza deliveryman, to get the word to him that his presence was required now. He didn't want to risk that.

He grasped the arm of a guard as he walked by. "I've got to go out for a few minutes. Tell Miss Gia I'll be back soon if she's looking for me."

"IT'S TAMBURO and the damn Peluso family. I know it is," Vito was saying to Gia in the library. "They've been trying to get their greedy hands on the family assets for years now."

Gia paced back and forth, feeling as if she was a "boo" away from jumping out of her skin.

What had made her think she was cut out for this? That she was emotionally and physically capable of carrying out a vendetta against those responsible for her father's death?

"I say we strike back."

Gia froze in the middle of the room and slowly turned to stare at Vito. "Certainly you're not suggesting that they were watching our men and purposely torched the entire restaurant with Joey in it after our guys left?"

He shrugged as if to say it wasn't outside the realm of possibility.

Gia thought it was too convenient and was reluctant to buy into the angry assumption.

Vito Cimino was old guard. He went way back with her father and had been instrumental in keeping them together after the first Venutos had established the family and through the four men who'd headed it since.

But being part of the old guard meant that he knew only the old ways.

There had to be a more effective means of dealing with matters of this nature.

"I say we need a meeting of the families."

Vito looked at her as if she'd lost a few biscotti during her pacing and that perhaps it wasn't too late to go back and pick them up. "There hasn't been a group meeting between the families in over a decade. It's too dangerous. The feds watch everything. Bringing the families together would give them the ammunition they need to prove we work together in some capacity. One goes down, we all go down."

"Well, then, I think a meeting is long overdue."

She tried to work the details out in her mind.

How quickly her plans had changed. First, she'd been interested in only bringing her father's killers to justice. Then she had gotten sucked into seeing to the family's day-to-day activities. Now she was proposing that she act in that leadership capacity in a full meeting with the other families.

Oh, she'd seen each of the family heads individually. But she needed to see them now, together, when everything was happening, to try to sort out who might have been behind the hit. Try to bait the guilty party into tipping his hand.

"Where's Luca?" she asked.

Vito shrugged and crossed his arms. "I don't know. One of the men said he left about an hour or so ago."

Where would Luca have had to go so suddenly?

No matter. She had work to do. Either with or without him.

LUCAS MADE IT back to the estate at around sunset. His handler hadn't wanted only to speak to him, he'd wanted a one-on-one, and those were harder to arrange than his sneaking out to his apartment for a telephone conversation.

So there they'd been, on New Jersey's east shore, watching boats and strolling with fishing gear as if they were factory workers out to bait a couple of hooks instead of agents trading information.

"Why didn't you send all the tapes?" his handler had asked.

He'd been told his name was John Smith. But since Lucas suspected that was an alias, he refused to get used to referring to him as such.

Smith was African-American and at least twice Lucas's age, his face bespeaking many years on the job. His eyes telling him that he knew something was up.

Lucas had pretended the question didn't surprise him. And it didn't. Not really. He'd known there would be inquiries into his change in behavior. He just hadn't known they'd come so soon and so directly.

"I had problems with my wire," he lied.

"Sporadic problems? The missing tapes aren't in one stretch but rather random, over a period of days."

"Trust me, you got everything that was important."

"Well, that's not for you to decide, is it? You're to send in everything you record."

"I did."

"That means you switched off the wire then. Why?"

He hadn't switched off the wire. Rather, he'd discarded the tapes that had included anything of importance he'd discussed with Gia. Anything that might incriminate her.

So far as Smith knew, there was no acting head of the Venuto crime family. With Lorenzo out of commission, and Giovanni dead, the FBI believed the family was in a chaotic sort of limbo waiting for the other shoe to drop. They might have their suspicions that Gia had taken over the reins. But he wasn't going to provide the proof that she had.

And he hoped he would never have to.

But in order to make that happen, he'd have to convince her to give up those same reins.

And judging by the other man across from him, and the escalating interest in his own activities, he wouldn't have long to do that.

"This wouldn't have anything to do with the past between you and Giovanna Trainello, would it?"

Lucas's movements slowed at the blatant question. He rarely heard Gia's given name used. It seemed to reveal her in an unflattering light, if only because the name was so similar to her father's.

"Didn't think we knew about that, did you?" Smith shook his head. "We know about a lot more than you'll ever suspect, Paretti. Why do you think we agreed to give you this undercover when you asked to be assigned to it? You used to be an insider, one of them."

Lucas turned his fishing pole as if to recast it. Yes, he used to be one of them. He'd never forget that. It had cost him his brother's life.

"But you're not now. Don't kid yourself into

thinking otherwise. All they have to do is catch a whiff of your association with the FBI and you'll join the list of other agents that share the same fate you will. Dead agents."

Lucas stared at him. "Are you threatening to expose me?"

"No, Paretti," he said as he pulled his own line in. "I'm promising I will if you don't do the job you were hired to do."

Now, as Lucas sat in his car in front of the Trainello house, he wondered what difference there was between the New York crime families and the bureau assigned to investigate them. The threat Smith had issued didn't sound all that different than a death warrant taken out by one of the families.

In fact, he was beginning to believe that gangs were gangs, no matter which way you sliced them. The mafia was a gang comprising Italian families connected to the homeland and their religion and their loyalty to each other. The FBI and NYPD and other agencies like them were gangs formed through training, but were no less formidable and ruthless when they wanted to be.

It seemed he had left one crime family to become a member of another.

But now it was Gia's life on the line.

GIA CURLED UP in her bed, a sketch pad open in her lap. She'd barely done more than scribble, but it was comforting somehow lying there, the scent of paper filling her nose along with the graphite from the pencil she held, the one lamp on the bedside table casting a golden glow about the dark room. The act of holding the pad lent an air of normalcy to her life that was sorely missing.

But if only for a few precious moments she wanted to forget about the armed men milling about the estate, her brother across the hall in a state of voluntary stupor, the details of the impending meeting with the other family heads.

And Luca.

She curved her bare feet more tightly under her. Or, rather, maybe she'd carved out the free time to give herself free sway to think about him.

Whenever she'd needed help in the past week, he'd been there, offering without being asked, lending her a hand up when she'd barely been aware she had fallen. She saw herself reflected in his big, blue eyes, and every time she began to feel dirty, somehow contaminated by the activities happening around her, the decisions she made, one look into his eyes and she saw that perhaps she couldn't be too bad. Not if he could still see her as something special, someone worth helping.

Perhaps even someone worth loving…again.

She gave up on her sketching and slapped the pad closed, the whoosh sounding loud in the quiet room. She put it on the nightstand next to the lamp and pushed the light covers off so she could get up. She stepped to the window overlooking the expansive backyard, remembering nights as a teenager when she would do the same thing. She barely registered the armed men walking around because they had been there when she was young, as well.

Could she and Luca still have a chance? Could the years that had gone between not be enough to cool embers that had burned too deep, too strong?

Could new love be enough to heal the scars that marred the old love?

Of course, she was no longer that lovestruck teen, but a grown woman not only capable of making her own decisions, but making weighty ones on which lives depended.

And him? To be sure, he was no longer the lanky twenty-four-year-old whose hair forever dipped over his right brow. And now experience and knowledge and wisdom loomed in his face.

As well as a deep desire for her.

Oh, she saw it. More than that, she felt it. There'd always existed a chemistry between them that transcended anything said or done or wished. Put them in the same room with other people, and the temperature rose ten degrees.

Put them in the same room alone and the air shimmered with the heat they gave off.

She shivered from the thought, battling against a longing that had taken on a life of its own.

Then again, she wasn't really battling it at all. Instead, she was reveling in it. Enjoying the hunger that pulsed deep in her belly. The tickle of awareness over her skin every time she thought about him.

She remembered their time together in the kitchen. Recalled the way she'd reacted when he'd withdrawn, spilling his seed over her thigh rather than inside her. It all seemed so long ago, yet could have happened mere moments before.

There was a brief knock at her door. She glanced down at her simple silk nightgown, making sure she was covered, and then called for whoever it was to enter.

She expected it to perhaps be one of Lorenzo's nurses, asking if she wanted anything more for the night.

Instead, she found herself staring at the man who had just been occupying her thoughts.

Luca.

GIA LOOKED LIKE an angel standing in front of the window. The lamplight outlined her slender shape under the white silk gown she wore, the fabric nearly transparent so that he could make out each of her curves.

Lucas wasn't sure what he'd expected. Probably that she'd be fully clothed sitting at the desk in the corner going over numbers of some sort or mapping out some intricate strategy on how to keep the family from harm.

Instead he found a woman ready for bed—or that had already been in bed, if the rumpled bedcovers were any indication—a sketch pad on the nightstand, as if she was waiting for her man to come home.

He tilted his head to the side, wondering. Had she been waiting for him to come back to the house?

He scanned her soft features and thought that she very well could have been. Welcome, relief and desire were all present in her face.

He quietly closed the door, staying right where he was, if only because he didn't trust himself to move closer. He needed to keep his wits about him. Remember what was going on around them.

Try to ignore what was developing between them.

"I just wanted to check in to see if everything was okay."

She smiled, stepping in his direction. "I'd ask where you went, but I'm not sure I'd like the answer."

Lucas avoided her gaze. She thought he might have been with another woman.

And, in essence, he had, hadn't he? His FBI contact was a person she wouldn't like him to be seeing. And by seeing him, he'd betrayed her. In the worst of all possible ways.

"Has anything happened while I've been gone?" he asked.

"Nothing that can't wait until morning," she answered, moving ever closer.

Every step she took made his pulse leap.

Damn, but she was beautiful.

"There are other things on my mind just now…"

12

LOOKING AT LUCA after spending so much time thinking about him was like being given a gift that was even better than she imagined.

Gia considered the way he stayed put near the door, as if he didn't trust himself to move closer…so she moved closer instead.

Perhaps it wasn't so much himself he couldn't trust, but her.

The silk of her gown moved against her skin, clinging to her sex, rasping against her hardened nipples. She watched as Luca's pupils grew wider at her seductive approach, the only part of him, it seemed, capable of moving at all.

She watched him swallow thickly. "Oh? And what do you have in mind?"

She laughed quietly, stopping directly in front of him, glad when she only smelled him and his subtle aftershave. No feminine perfume, no cigarette smoke. Just one hundred percent pure, fine Luca Paretti.

"What I have in mind can't be expressed in words," she murmured, taking his hand and running her fingers over the back. "It's better shown."

She pressed his palm down over her left breast, holding it there, willing him to feel the thundering of her heartbeat just beneath the surface.

His expression grew fiercer.

"Gia, I'm not so sure…"

"Shh," she said, pressing the finger of her free hand against his lips to prevent him from saying more. "No more words."

She took her hand back and used it to push the strap of her gown so that it slid over her shoulder, slipping the fabric down between his hand and her breast. A small, strangled sound escaped his throat.

Gia trembled in response.

She followed with the other strap so that the material whispered to the floor in a silken puddle. She was nude underneath. She watched Luca appreciate that little fact, taking her in with his heavy-lidded gaze.

Then he did exactly as she expected, hoped he might: he groaned and swept her up into his arms, carrying her to the bed just steps away. Gia clutched his shoulders, feeling lighter than the feather he made of her. Once she was on top of the soft bedding, she released him and scooted farther up, keeping her legs enticingly together.

"Gia, you're going to be the death of me."

He yanked at his tie impatiently, and then his jacket, his jerky movements speaking of an urgency that reflected the same that filled her stomach. It was taking longer than she would have liked, so she drew up on her knees to help him, not expecting his sudden kiss.

So hot...so demanding.

The attention of his mouth took her breath away as he hauled her to him, his clothes still half on, the material of his suit jacket chafing her nipples even as he yanked it off, never breaking contact with her lips.

Gia thrust her fingers into his thick hair, holding on for dear life as he kissed her like she was water and he had just traversed the Sahara. All too soon, he broke the contact and pressed her back against the mattress, his erection thick and hard between her legs, not breaching her portal, but rather cradled between her engorged flesh.

She gasped and tried to force entry. He drew away, staring deep into her eyes, as if something had just occurred to him.

"It's because I withdrew, isn't it?" he asked,

surprising her with his sudden insight. "That's the reason you went cold on me the last time."

Gia gazed at him, so hot she was afraid she was at risk of self-combusting. "Shh…"

He shook his head. "No. I don't want it to happen again, Gia. I won't share something special with you and have you turn away from me again. I won't."

She ran her hand down his abdomen and then wrapped her fingers around his long, thick erection, squeezing. He groaned and caught her wrist.

He kissed her deeply, not speaking again until she panted with need. "I didn't have protection then. I don't have it now. Are you willing to take the risk of getting pregnant?"

She stared up into his eyes, his skin burning her fingers, his hand tight on hers. "Are you?"

He didn't say anything for a long moment. Merely gazed at her intently. "I'd be honored if you'd have my child."

Gia released her grip on his manhood and curved her arms around his back, holding him tight, holding him close.

The past crashed back like a thousand storm-tossed waves. She fought to keep it at bay, but she was helpless against the torrent of emotion.

"What is it?" Luca whispered when she went

still, forcing her to move from where her face was tucked into his shoulder. "Gia, what happened? What's the matter?"

She shook her head, helpless to stop the tears streaming down her cheeks, the emotions from wracking her body. "Nothing. It doesn't matter now. What I needed to hear, you just told me."

"It matters if it has the power to bring you to tears. Tell me, *cara*. Do you want to become pregnant? Is that what this is about?"

Gia bit hard on her bottom lip and closed her eyes, unprepared for the Italian endearment or his sensitivity. How could she possibly tell him the reason why she'd been upset when he withdrew the other night? Share what had been a secret for so long she didn't even know if she could utter the words?

She recalled the morning she found out as if it had happened today, standing in the bathroom staring at the indicator stick. Pregnant.

And Luca was gone.

How did she now convey to him the depth of emotion she'd felt? How elated she'd been at the thought that their lovemaking had resulted in the creation of a baby? Their baby?

How did she tell him how afraid she'd been

when she was unable to contact him, find out where he was?

How utterly alone she'd felt, alone with no mother to offer her advice?

Oh, God.

She hadn't been able to tell her father or brothers for fear of what they might do to Luca.

And Luca had never known because she'd never had a chance to tell him.

He shifted on top of her, moving to sit on the side of the bed, his back to her. "Sweet Jesus…don't tell me…"

Was it her overwhelmed reaction to his saying he'd be honored if she bore his child? Or were they still plugged in on a level she didn't think she would ever completely understand? She didn't know how he'd guessed, but she suspected that he had.

She'd had no choice but to terminate the pregnancy.

"It doesn't matter now," she whispered fervently, wanting so much for her words to be true that she ached with it. "It happened a long time ago."

But it did matter. It would always matter. She would forever struggle with the morality of her actions. There wasn't a day that went by when she didn't remember what it was like to know she was pregnant with Luca's baby. The joy. The happiness. The hope for the future.

But everything changed during a procedure so routine to the doctor and the nurses who performed it that the entire experience emerged surreal.

Luca looked at her over his shoulder. "But I'm just now learning about it, so it might as well be happening now."

Gia felt suddenly, inexplicably exposed. She drew the top sheet up over her breasts, covering herself.

"Was it a boy or a girl?"

She clamped her eyes closed, but they did nothing to stop the flow of tears. "I don't know. They refused to tell me."

Again, nothing but the sound of his deep breathing and her stifled sniffles.

"How old would he or she be now?"

"Six...last month."

"Dear Lord in heaven." Luca dropped his head into his hands, as if the information was too much for him to bear.

It was then that Gia knew a fear she hadn't considered before. A fear that he might hate her for aborting his child.

She desperately searched for something to say to him. Some way to make him look at her again as he had just moments before. Before he'd learned the truth.

"I didn't know where you were. I didn't know how to find you. I went to your parents and begged them to have you call me. I waited to hear something. Almost too long." She swallowed back a sob. "I didn't know what to do. I couldn't tell my father... I couldn't tell anyone...

"And you were just...gone..."

Gia's very bones seemed to disintegrate and she no longer possessed the power to sit up.

But before her back hit the sheets, Luca was scooping her up into his arms, draping her across his lap and holding her so tightly she couldn't breathe.

"Oh, Gia, what have I done to you? Oh, sweet Gia..."

His words were her complete undoing as she collapsed against him, wanting, needing to lose herself in his embrace.

She'd feared his hatred. She'd received his love.

Gia was sure of that. And in that one moment, knew that he had always loved her. He'd left not because of her, but because of reasons not connected to her. His brother's death had left him searching for answers his wandering could only provide.

Unfortunately that same wandering had left her alone and pregnant. And she'd made the only decision she could.

There wasn't a moment that went by that she didn't remember that day. Didn't lament it. Didn't think about how old their child would be now and whether it would have been a boy or a girl.

But now that she'd finally told him, it was as if he'd realized the almost unbearable burden weighing down her shoulders, and had lifted at least half of it to put on his.

He threaded his fingers through her hair and drew her closer, gazing deep into her eyes, sadness in the depths of his. "I'm so, so sorry you had to go through that by yourself, Gia. So very sorry I wasn't there for you. For our child."

And then he kissed her.

LUCAS'S HEART beat thickly in his chest. He was filled with love for this woman who had been forced to ignore her own heart in order to make a decision no one should have to make alone. He was filled with hatred that he had been so consumed by vengeance for his brother's death that he'd lost his own child.

He couldn't seem to kiss Gia long enough,

deeply enough, to assuage the need and guilt gnawing at him from the inside out. She tasted of heaven even though she'd been through a hell he feared he'd never completely understand. He'd known something was wrong with her that night in the kitchen. Had suspected she'd gone through changes he couldn't begin to fathom, when he'd first seen her again after so many years.

He'd had no idea how deep her pain had gone.

And now he shared that pain.

He caressed her bare shoulders, needing to pull her closer, yet keep her far enough away so that he might touch her. Her breasts were warm, her nipples rigid. He bent his head to take the right one into his mouth, laving it, wishing the experience could prove a salve to both their damaged souls. He'd betrayed her. He'd betrayed himself. And she had no idea the lengths to which he had betrayed her…was still betraying her.

Guilt pulsed through him.

Gia rested against the sheets, more beautiful than a sculpture of Venus come to life. Lucas reached down between them and gently probed her damp curls, burrowing through them to find her moist center. He sought and found the bit of flowering flesh at the apex of her womanhood and pinched it lightly, satisfied with her sharp gasp. Then he parted her thighs, spreading her legs wide with his knee. The new openness allowed him access to her sex and he took immediate advantage, stroking her and then fingering the edges of her before inserting his finger deep inside her slick flesh.

She was tight and wet and oh so ready for him. She shifted restlessly against the bed, so near climax that he knew all he would have to do was stroke her G-spot and she'd melt into a puddle. Only he didn't want her to go that way. He wanted to be with her when she came. He wanted...no, needed, to reach that plateau with her. They'd experienced too much already separately.

He moved his other knee between her legs and grasped his erection, stroking her with the turgid length. Her juices covered him, lubricating his skin, preparing him for entrance. Gia reached up and anchored herself with her hands against his shoulders as he positioned the wide tip against her and entered her slightly before withdrawing. She protested with a thrust of her hips upward, forcing him deeper inside.

Lucas sank in to the hilt, not stopping until his pubis met with hers.

Gia shuddered around him, the contraction of

her muscles as they adjusted to his thick girth nearly shoving him over the edge. He gritted his back teeth, his heartbeat moving from his chest to his swollen penis. His erection twitched inside her as he slowly withdrew, then surged again, stroking her as intimately as a man could a woman.

Desperate to show her through actions, not words, how much he loved her.

And he did love her, didn't he? Had never stopped loving her. She was still the beautiful young woman who'd looked at him with stars in her eyes, despite the despair she'd suffered at his hands.

And she, miracle of miracles, still loved him.

He didn't know what he'd done to deserve her love. Didn't want to think too much on the topic lest he find himself undeserving of it. All he knew was a roaring urgency to connect with her on a level he'd never connected with another person in his life.

He stroked her again…and again. Listening as her breathing grew more labored, her breasts heaving from the effort it took to draw air into her constricted lungs. Having trouble getting enough air himself.

He skimmed his hand over her breasts, then down over her side, not stopping until he'd curved it under her softly rounded bottom, parting her wider from behind. His thrusts grew more demanding, melding his sex with hers, his soul reaching out for hers.

And she offered it up to him in a burst of shimmering gold passion.

13

THE FOLLOWING MORNING Lucas stood staring out the French doors in the kitchen at the back grounds. The sun was just now rising, but he'd been up for hours. Had left Gia asleep in her bed at around four to come downstairs and try to make sense of what had happened in the past few weeks…what had happened seven years ago.

It seemed as if within the blink of an eye his life had been altered. His entire existence transformed with a few whispered words from Gia's mouth.

She'd been pregnant with his child.

He dry washed his face with his hands, regretting that he hadn't tried to get some rest. But he knew he wouldn't have been able to close his eyes. There was too much to think about. Too much to consider.

And if the emotional matters weren't enough, he had to reflect on the current legal storm cloud hanging over the Trainello house. It was only a matter of time before the authorities came back with a warrant for Vito's—or worse, Gia's— arrest for the death of Joey Guarino. How might she stand up then?

In his training at Quantico, he'd not only learned how to use certain techniques to get suspects to talk. He'd been broken himself, when he'd been convinced no one would be able to torture anything from him. It was said he had taken longer than any other bureau trainee, but he'd learned an important lesson that day: that everyone broke, eventually. All the inquisitor had to do was find the right stimulus.

In his case, his questioner had used his brother to bring him to his emotional knees after two days of using various torture methods, appealing to his anger in his weakened state to get access to what he was looking for.

Of course, in the case of the New York City prosecutor's office, they were legally prevented from employing most methods used by the FBI, but that didn't stop Lucas from wanting to protect Gia from any questioning whatsoever.

And he needed to devise a way to stop it.

He hadn't had to worry about Claudio Lancione's murder. Nobody cared about a known hit man ending up in the East River. But a well-known restaurant owner was another matter entirely, despite his ties to the mob.

He heard voices in the other room. He put his coffee cup down and went in search of them. Vito, probably, up and ready for another day.

He halted in the doorway to the foyer. It was, indeed, Vito. He was talking to a man Lucas didn't recognize. And as part of his undercover job, he had the 411 on everyone closely associated to the Trainello family, and by extension, the Venuto crime family.

The man was probably about his age, but looked at least a decade older because of his thick, pockmarked skin and a little extra weight that was pure muscle, probably because of weight lifting.

Vito spotted Lucas and he whispered something to the man, who promptly left.

"You're up early," Vito said by way of greeting. "Have you made coffee yet?"

He passed him and walked into the kitchen and Lucas followed.

"I'll pour you a cup," Lucas said, going about it. "Who were you just talking to?"

Vito didn't say anything.

"Nothing related to the law yesterday?"

"No, no. Nothing like that."

Lucas already suspected as much. But he was curious as to why Vito didn't offer more.

Over the past year he'd spent working under-cover with the Trainellos, he still knew his position was precarious. Vito had never much liked him, for reasons he apparently preferred to keep to himself. And that personal wariness had carried over into professional affairs. There was a great deal that Lucas wasn't privy to, no matter how he tried like hell to make it otherwise.

Vito Cimino was true to the old way. He trusted no one. Not even his own mother, as it was said. And that wariness had stood him in good stead with Giovanni Trainello.

It also made it impossible to nail him for any wrongdoing.

"I have some things I need to get from my office," Lucas said. "Should Gia ask, tell her I'll return later this morning."

Vito nodded. "I'll do that."

But as Lucas walked away, the tiny hairs on the back of his neck prickled in alert and he knew that something had changed. A danger-ous wind seemed to blow in through the door he opened and swirl around inside the Trai-nello house.

And he couldn't help feeling as if he was the one responsible for letting it in.

GIA TOOK her breakfast in Lorenzo's room. She kept up the hope that normal activity would bring him around.

The ritual was more enjoyable in her mother's old bedroom than it had been in Lorenzo's. Her mother had liked beautiful things and her room boasted a bowed window seat where Gia had one of the nurses set up a table on which she could place the tray she brought up. A nurse followed with a similar tray for her brother filled with all his favorites. Up until now, he hadn't even blinked at the offerings. But this morning, she'd requested the nurse only inject half his usual pain medication into the intravenous tube. So when his breakfast was put on the retractable table in front of him, he shifted and made a face.

"Good morning, Lorenzo," she said from her spot on the window seat, picking up her coffee and sipping it. "Maria fixed eggs Benedict this morning." She made an exaggerated sniffing sound. "Smells delicious."

He cracked open his eyes, squinting at the tray before him and then slowly turning his head toward her. He raised a hand to shield his eyes. Gia adjusted the blinds so the sunlight wasn't shining directly on him.

"Welcome back to the land of the living."

He made a few swallowing sounds. The nurse fed him ice chips. He waved her away after eating a few. "I'd prefer to be dead."

Gia pretended that his words were of no mind to her, although they sliced through her heart. "But you're not. So you're just going to have to deal with it until you're well enough to see to the task yourself."

"What did you do to my drugs?"

"After being on them for so long, your tolerance is probably greater, so my guess is that your regular dose isn't as effective as it was."

"Then increase it."

Gia took a bite of eggs and forced it down her throat as if it were the best thing she'd ever eaten. It tasted like chalk. "Sorry, but you'll have to talk to your doctor about that."

"Call him in."

"You have an appointment for later this afternoon."

"Fuck the afternoon." He raised his hand and it fell on top of his tray, upsetting a glass of juice there, the lack of use of the limb lessening his power over it. He swept the entire tray from the table in frustration. "Call him in now."

Gia sipped her coffee and then shook her head. "No can do. He's booked solid for the morning."

"Then unbook him."

"I'd really like to, but—"

"You did this, didn't you? You lowered my dose, that's why I'm awake now."

Gia finished chewing a bite and swallowed with slow deliberation before wiping her mouth with her napkin. She rose from the window seat so that she stood next to her brother's bed.

"What's the date today, Lorenzo?"

He blinked at her. "What?"

"You heard me. If you can tell me today's date, I'll have the nurse increase your medication."

He blinked at her, only half-lucid. For which she was glad, because she was afraid of what he might do if he was completely awake.

"Fuck you."

"No, fuck you, Lorenzo. Today is Thursday, August 22. You've slept for almost six weeks solid. Save for those times when you had to meet with the doctor to increase your medication."

"I'm in pain, damn it! Don't you understand that?"

"Are you?" She reached over and took his

hand and then turned it over in hers. She piched the skin there. He jerked his hand away.

"What are you doing? Playing doctor now, little sis?"

"No. I'm just trying to get my brother back."

"Yes, well, your brother is not available at the moment." He'd turned his head to gaze through the window, taking in where her breakfast still sat, barely eaten.

"Well, could you please tell me when he will be available?" she asked quietly, trying to keep the edge of desperation from her voice. "Because I really need him right now. Things are falling apart around my ears because I've been doing the job he was meant to do. The job he was raised to do. And I'm afraid that the next thing that I do on his behalf will see us all killed."

"It's no less than I deserve."

"And me?" she whispered.

He looked at her then, and for the first time in a month and a half she viewed something other than self-pity.

"Do you want me to die, Lorenzo?"

"You're not going to die."

"Aren't I? What, am I invincible? If that's the case, then maybe you'll want to tell Gino Guarino that after an order I made resulted in his brother

Joey being killed. Or how about Tamburo, who'd like nothing better than to see me hanging from a meat hook? Because right now I don't have a clue how to change any of it. Do you?"

He looked away.

Gia took his hand again. "You're all I have left in this world, Lorenzo. Please come back to me. Come back to the family."

He jerked his hand a second time as if the pain of her words was greater than her earlier pinch. "Nurse! Get the doctor on the phone. Now!"

The nurse looked to her.

"What are you waiting for?" Lorenzo demanded.

The young woman cleared her throat. "For Miss Gia to confirm the order."

"Miss Gia…" Lorenzo stared at her. "So you're Miss Gia now?"

"In my brother's absence, I'm the head of this household."

"Then give her the order."

"I'll do no such thing. The doctor will be here this afternoon."

Lorenzo glared at her.

Gia walked toward the door. "Oh, and by the way? After he's done with you, he'll be talking to me. And I'm going to tell him to start reducing your medication."

"You bitch. You wouldn't dare."

Gia knew it was the lack of medication and his dependency on it that was causing him to be so crass and cutting. But it didn't lessen the hurt his words caused. "I would and I will," Gia said, even though her heart was breaking in her chest. "You're still alive, Lorenzo, like it or not. And it's about damn time you started acting like it."

She walked into the hall, closing the door after her and the nurse who followed. The vase of fresh roses that she had arranged to be placed on Lorenzo's nightstand every morning crashed against the closed wood. Gia flinched, trying to quell the flow of tears that threatened.

"WHERE'S LUCA?" Gia asked Vito a little while later, after having composed herself.

She'd found the older man in her father's office taking a meeting with one of the higher lieutenants.

Vito dismissed the lieutenant and didn't answer until after the man had left the room. "He went out. He'll be back later this morning."

Gia caught herself with her hand against her chest and removed it.

Ever since waking up this morning she'd

wanted to see him again. Verify that what she thought had happened last night, had. She'd felt lighter than she had in a long, long time. And recognized that part of the reason was that she'd finally told Luca a truth she'd kept hidden from him for far too long.

A truth that would always be a bruise against the love that they shared. But that had made them realize that that love still existed.

"What time is the meeting today?" she asked.

She didn't have to specify to which meeting she was referring. There was only one meeting on her agenda. And that was with the four other heads of the New York mafia crime families.

"One o'clock."

She nodded, hoping that Luca would be back in time to attend with her. In the midst of everything that had happened last night, she hadn't had an opportunity to tell him about the meeting.

"You can still cancel," Vito said.

She looked at him. "Why would I want to do that? It's the only way I'm going to find out who was behind my father's and brother's hit." She absently hugged herself. "And hopefully stop all this from escalating into full-out war."

14

"I WANT YOU to pull the locals off Miss Trainello," Lucas said from the confines of his safe
room in Queens.

He waited for his handler to respond. Which
didn't appear to be something he was interested
in immediately doing.

"Smith, did you hear me?"

"I know I ordered you to get closer to the
subject, Paretti, but it sounds like you're getting
a little too close."

"You don't know what you're talking about."

"Tell me about the meeting today."

Alarm bells went off in Lucas's head. "What
meeting?"

A prolonged silence and then, "Another
example of you withholding information from
us? Or are you genuinely in the dark? Either way,
such a major development doesn't reflect well on
your investigative abilities."

"What meeting, damn it?"

"Our inside with Tamburo says that a meeting has been requested between all family heads for today at one. And that your girl Giovanna is the one who asked for it."

"Jesus…"

Lucas rang off, grabbed his jacket and rushed from the room, ignoring the chirping phone as he slammed the door behind him.

WHAT DID ONE WEAR to a meeting with four of the most dangerous men in New York City?

Gia recognized the question as frivolous and blamed it on her nerves as she straightened her black jacket with white piping over black pants and made sure her white blouse wasn't bunching around her breasts. She couldn't remember a time when she'd been this anxious. Not even when she and Bryan had appeared at their first major fashion show and had three of their models come down with the stomach flu an hour before they were to hit the runway.

Of course, the difference between the two events was that while all participants might want to kill each other, in the case of the mob bosses, they didn't hesitate to act on their desires.

There was a knock at her bedroom door. After

calling out, Frankie cracked it open. "The car is waiting, Miss Gia."

When wasn't it waiting? But she didn't say the words. She merely thanked her assistant, took the briefcase he handed her and then preceded him out into the hall, down the stairs and outside, where he opened the door to the car for her.

For security reasons, Vito was riding in a separate vehicle that would follow hers.

Gia glanced around. She didn't have to wonder what she was looking for. She knew. Luca.

She hadn't seen him all morning. And the thought of attending this meeting scared the hell out of her.

Frankie hesitated. "Is there anything else you need, Miss Gia?"

She smiled at him and sat back in the black leather seat, slipping on her Dior sunglasses. "No, thank you, Frankie. That will be all."

"All right, then." He closed the door and stood back.

The late-model black Mercedes smoothly pulled away from the curb.

When she'd requested the meeting yesterday, she hadn't expected that the others would be agreeable to it, or that it would come about so quickly. She guessed that the reason for the first part was that the other heads probably hoped she'd name the person set to inherit the Venuto family holdings. Because nobody, including her, believed she'd take the land for long....

As for the second, the sooner they gathered and dispersed, the worse for any feds or local law enforcement that might want in on the meeting themselves.

Gia reached for her briefcase and looked in the front pocket of her designer bag for her cell phone. It wasn't there. She searched the rest of the compartments and inside, only then realizing that she must have left it at the house.

She sighed and reached for the car phone. "What's the number for the phone in Vito's car?" she asked the driver.

He told her.

She punched it in and then sat back, watching as the Mercedes headed farther out in Long Island rather than inland, the remote location of the meeting at mob boss John Mangano's estate allowing for a moderate margin of safety from law enforcement.

Or for a secluded place to dump the bodies of those not left standing.

Gia swallowed thickly. "Yes, Vito, it's Gia. Have you heard anything from Luca?"

"No. Haven't you?"

"No."

"At the risk of sounding like a broken Sinatra record, I just want to tell you one last time that it's still not too late to cancel."

"Thanks, Vito. I'll see you there."

She disconnected the extension and then called Frankie for Luca's cell number.

"You want me to patch you through, Miss Gia?" he asked, having recently begun to learn the phone system.

She hesitated. Her mind really should be on the impending meeting, not Luca. But somehow she couldn't ignore the small pang in her stomach that was growing into a larger one.

Where was he?

LUCAS WATCHED the expensive cars pull in to the multicar garage of the Mangano estate one by one. He hadn't had time to get out to the Trainello house before Gia left, so he'd come straight to the meeting place. He knew he was taking a huge risk since the only ones who would know where the meeting was were Gia and Vito.

He only hoped that one or the other of them didn't figure out that neither of them had told him.

Gia got out of the back of the next Mercedes

that pulled in, looking directly at him and smiling…before she spotted the dozen or so men armed with automatic weapons posted around the garage.

"Thank God you're here," she said quietly as she came to stand next to him.

Vito had exited his vehicle and joined them, eyeing Lucas with open interest.

Vincenzo Tamburo was the next to join them.

"Gentlemen?" a man in a white suit with a black tie said from the doorway. "And lady," he added with a nod in Gia's direction. "Everyone is assembled. If you'll follow me."

"What is this about?" Vincenzo asked Vito as they walked.

Gia shared a glance with Lucas.

"Miss Gia called the meeting against my advice," Vito said.

They reached the door and Lucas stepped aside to allow Gia to go first, realizing only after she passed that chivalry probably was moot in present company.

He followed after her, cutting off Vito when he tried to elbow in. Let the old man make of his actions what he would. He wasn't going to give him a chance to ask her what he was doing there.

As he saw it, his cover was a thread away from being blown, anyway.

As he looked around the room packed with countless men that topped the FBI's most wanted list, his only wish was that it would happen after the meeting.

As was the custom during such meetings, a traditional Italian meal was being served up to the participants. Lucas guessed it was because the Italians believed that everyone got along better and thought more clearly on a full stomach.

The sight of the men already seated forking pasta into their mouths as they glared at the latest arrivals chased away whatever was left of his own appetite.

As expected, he'd been frisked upon his arrival, the only arms present left behind in the garage along with the goons from the various families. This was also done on purpose. Essentially it guaranteed that should the meeting not go well, gunfire wouldn't break out.

At least not from inside the room that was little more than an extended garage.

He pulled out a chair for Gia while Vito took the seat on the other side of her. He noted with interest that rather than take the seat next to Vito, Tamburo opted for one on the other side of the tables that had been set up in a U formation so that everyone could see everybody else.

He and Gia didn't refuse the offered dinner but neither of them made more than a perfunctory show of eating any of it. There was some conversation between the others present, but the hushed tones spoke more of unease than camaraderie.

Not surprising. Lucas was lightly surprised the room could contain the egos of the city's largest crime families.

Five minutes into the meal, Vincenzo Tamburo broke the proverbial ice.

"The reason behind this meeting had better be important, Gia. The families haven't met in one room in over a decade. With good reason," he said, wiping his mouth and putting his napkin down on top of his own barely touched plate.

The gesture wasn't a comment on the quality of the food. Because even though Lucas's taste buds were a bit distracted, even he noted that the pasta and marinara sauce was excellent.

Lucas watched Gia square her shoulders. "The reason is valid. And I expect that each of you would have done the same if you were facing the same questions I am."

"With all due respect," John Mangano said, indicating that what he was about to say would lack all respect. "Shouldn't your brother, Lorenzo, be the one calling this meeting?"

Gia stared him and then each of his fellow family heads down one by one, ignoring their seconds in command and any others they had brought along. "Since I'm the current leader of the Venuto family, it's my duty to attend to such matters."

"Why did you order a hit on Guarino?" one of the members wanted to know.

The question prompted several like questions and comments around the table, Joey Guarino's death apparently having hit a nerve.

"That's a Venuto family matter," Gia said. "And it will be handled accordingly."

Tamburo snorted as he put down his wineglass, appearing to be enjoying the proceedings so far. "That's the reason why I and my brothers—" he gestured toward the others "—agreed to this farce of a meeting. Because as far as we're concerned, there is no Venuto family anymore. Additionally...the Guarinos are no longer members of the Venuto family." His thick chest puffed out. "They came on board with the Pelusos last week."

Lucas noted Gia's well-handled shock. The desired dissolution of the Venuto family wasn't new...but that the Guarinos had signed on with Tamburo was.

Thankfully a couple of the other family heads disagreed with Tamburo's latter statement.

"The Guarinos are with us," Mangano said, his silverware hitting his plate with a clatter.

"Joey Guarino's death was an accident—" Gia had to raise her voice to be heard over the hubbub "—brought about by the refusal to honor a family debt. A debt Gino has now made good on."

Everyone quietly considered her. She cleared her throat and went on.

"The remaining Guarino, I was assured just this morning, is still very much a part of the Venuto family. A family that still exists and is as strong as ever under my guidance." She crossed her hands and laid them on the table in place of the plate that had been removed. "And any more suggestions to the contrary will be taken as a threat to the family's autonomy and treated as such."

John Mangano's chair legs scraped against the painted concrete floor. "Are you sure about what you're saying, little girl? Are you making a declaration of war?"

Gia looked at him directly. "I'm saying that I and the family will not tolerate or accept anyone else's disrespect from here on out." She paused. "And I haven't been anyone's little girl for over a month and a half since my father was killed. By someone in this room."

There was much exchanging of gazes, but silence reigned.

"So what did you call this friggin' meeting for?" Tamburo wanted to know, his meaty face turning an unhealthy shade of red.

"I called this meeting for a very good reason. I don't care how, I don't care why, but I want one of you to tell me who was ultimately responsible for the death of my father and my brother Mario. And I want him dealt with accordingly."

15

OUTWARDLY, GIA MIGHT look like a cool operator. Inwardly, her heart beat a million miles a minute.

But what had to be done had to be done. And she was tired of being given the runaround, having roadblocks thrown up in her face, and being treated like the little girl Mangano had called her.

Her father and brother had been killed. And she intended to make the man responsible for the hit pay.

Mangano looked to Vito. "You support Gia in this, Vito?"

Gia glanced at the older man seated two chairs down from her.

"Vito's presence at this table next to the Venuto family head should speak for itself," Luca said instead.

Gia looked at him and her heartbeat calmed a bit. The thought of facing the families without him had nearly sent her into a state of panic. But she realized she would have been fine even if he hadn't shown up at the meet. She supposed she had Vito to thank, no matter how opposed to this meeting he'd been, for inviting Luca.

Then again, just knowing Luca was beside her, and behind her, gave her a courage she hadn't known she possessed until that moment.

There was a loud clap outside the room that sounded ominously like gunfire. Gia stared in the direction of the doorway, only realizing that the sound had come from the opposite direction, more specifically from the windows behind her.

Another shot and the glass shattered.

"Get down!" Lucas shouted, grabbing her and nearly body slamming her to the concrete floor while everyone scrambled for cover, the room erupting in chaos.

"Are you hit?"

Gia couldn't do more than stare up into Luca's face, so close to hers it was little more than a blur. She couldn't seem to draw a breath.

"Damn it, Gia, have you been shot?"

She slowly blinked at him as more gunfire sounded, probably in response to the first gunman.

Lucas opened her jacket and then turned her over.

Gia finally snapped out of it and righted herself. "I'm fine. I haven't been hit."

The other heads scrambled for the entrance to the connecting garage and their cars, the ones nearer the door already squealing away from the enclosure in their limos and Mercedes.

Luca hauled her away from the window and she watched as Vito ducked through the door into the garage.

"Do you think you were the target?" Luca asked, not trusting her words and still giving her a thorough check-over.

"I don't know," she said, staring at something on the other side of the room. "But if I was, they got the wrong person." She swallowed hard. "Or did they get the right one?"

Luca turned to see to what she was referring. And he sank to the floor next to her as he took in the sight.

Vincenzo Tamburo was still sitting in his chair, leaning slightly backward, his eyes wide open and unseeing. He had been shot in the middle of the forehead, a thin trail of blood trickling down over his brow. On the wall behind him was a red spot the size of a Frisbee.

Gia's stomach lurched as she realized it was the back of his head.

"Come on," Luca said, hauling her to her feet. "Let's get out of here."

It was the best idea she had heard all day.

LUCAS SAT next to Gia, longing to touch her but not daring to, as her car headed the half hour inland toward the Trainello estate. For a few precious minutes she'd allowed him to hold her close, but once they were well away from the meeting site, she'd slid away from him to the far side of the seat and sat staring through the window.

He felt powerless to reach out to her, to allay her fears. He couldn't even contact his handler and ask if he knew what in the hell had gone down at the meeting site.

All he could feel was gratitude that Gia was all right.

And anger at himself for not having been there to prevent her from going to the meeting at all.

What had she been thinking? While he admitted that she'd handled herself not only admirably, but commandingly, no one entered into such a meeting to make demands of people the likes of Tamburo and his fellow family heads. Not as a junior head yourself. And not when you had yet to be accepted as the legitimate head of the largest family that everyone had their sights on.

Common sense told him that he should have driven back in his own car rather than having the help see that it was returned to the estate. Right now he could have been placing a call to the emergency line for his handler and been setting things in motion to confirm his suspicions on who the shooter was and who he was working for. Pass on that Tamburo had been hit. By a bullet possibly meant for Gia.

Instead he'd chosen to drive with her, needing to be by her side in case she wanted him. Needing to convince himself that she had, indeed, made it through unscathed.

While he had chosen Gia over his job a few times the past couple of weeks, he had never done so in a situation of this magnitude. And now that he had, he wondered where that left him in terms of his job. Because after everything that had happened, he knew only one thing for certain: he would choose Gia every time.

GIA SAT BACK in the car's seat feeling numb. For some reason she couldn't pinpoint, the last conversation she'd had with her father surfaced in her mind, barely managing to eclipse the afternoon's events.

She'd last seen Giovanni Trainello the Sunday

before he was murdered when he'd come to her Manhattan apartment for dinner. It was a rare occasion when he left the safety of his estate and Gia had made sure she'd cooked all of his favorites, relishing having her father in her environs rather than her being in his.

"You're going to make someone a great wife one day, Giovanna," he'd commented with pride after having taken his last bite of gelato and wiping his mouth with a napkin. "Speaking of which, are there any candidates you might want to introduce me to?"

Gia had laughed as she poured them self a cup of coffee. "No, there aren't."

He'd made a tsking sound. "Shame. What are you? Twenty-six now? By twenty-six, your mother and I had been married for seven years and we'd already had all three of you kids."

Gia had known that, of course, but she'd never applied the knowledge to her own life. Only a couple of decades ago, women had gotten married younger, had their families younger. Nowadays it was different.

Still, somehow it had struck her that she had been nineteen when Luca left.

Had he stayed...

She looked at him now, even as more of her father's words filled her mind.

"You know I don't buy into any of that romantic love-at-first-sight horse crap, Giovanna," he'd said, and Gia had laughed, because her mother had always said that her father was the most romantic man she'd met. "But I do believe that when you meet that one person meant for you, you'll know it. This is true. Because it happened to me. I knew it the moment I met your mother that she would be my wife. And no matter what, even if I had known what would happen down the road, that I would lose her to cancer, I wouldn't have changed anything if I could."

Gia had sipped her coffee, considering him over the rim of the cup. "Is there somewhere you're going with this conversation, Papa?"

He'd leaned back in his chair. "No, no. Nowhere in particular. I was just wondering if maybe the reason you haven't found your husband yet is that you're being too picky."

She'd raised a brow at that. "Picky?"

"Uh-huh. Like maybe you expect too much from a man." He'd leaned forward then, clasping his hands on the tablecloth. "Remember a man, any man, is only human. Imperfect. It's the way we're made. There are going to be things about him that maybe you don't like. That maybe you don't want to know."

A shadow had passed over his eyes and she realized he was again talking about his relationship with her mother.

"But that don't mean he won't love you. And that you can't love him." He'd waggled his finger at her then. "Remember that."

Gia wasn't sure why she'd recalled the conversation so clearly. Possibly because it was the last time he'd spoken to her before he was gunned down in cold blood.

Possibly because she'd nearly joined him in the family burial plot a little while ago.

"Gia?" Luca said softly, gently cupping her face and rubbing his thumb along her cheekbone. "Are you all right?"

She nodded her head and leaned into him. "I'm fine."

Her response referred to more than just her physical state. It reflected what was going on in her heart.

Because she knew with certainty that no matter his flaws, no matter what had gone before, Luca was the one man in the entire world meant exclusively for her.

No matter what.

16

"Aren't you coming in?"

Gia stood on the top step of her father's house and faced Lucas where he had stopped on the first.

Her nerves were raw and she still feared she might be sick to her stomach. She needed more than anything to make sense out of everything that had happened. And she'd prefer to do that with Lucas by her side.

"There's someone I need to see first," he said quietly, his gaze steady on hers, intense.

He stepped up so that he could kiss her lingeringly.

"I'll be back before you miss me."

Gia watched him walk to the first car in line in the driveway and get in, silently telling him that she missed him already.

She turned and walked inside the house, expecting the familiar surroundings to provide her with peace.

Instead, she felt worse. Unsafe.

Men milled about everywhere. Gia touched the sleeve of one as he passed. "What's going on?"

Had something happened here as well as at the meeting site?

"Mr. Cimino ordered us to lock down the place," he told her and then continued on his mission.

Gia went in search of Vito. When she didn't find him in the library where he usually was, she went to her office. She was surprised to find the door locked.

That was funny. She'd thought she was the only one with a key.

She knocked twice but didn't receive an answer.

Frankie popped up next to her. "Mr. Cimino is in there with some man in a suit."

Gia frowned. All the men around the estate wore suits. "How do you mean?"

"Someone official looking."

"Like the police?"

"I don't know. The guy just didn't look like anyone I'm used to seeing."

"Thanks, Frankie."

She raised her hand to knock again.

"Do you want some coffee or something?"

Gia smiled. The kid seemed completely oblivious to the frenetic activity around him. "Sure, Frankie. That would be nice."

He hurried down the hall.

She knocked again, but before she could call out to Vito, the door opened inward. She moved aside as the suited man Frankie had referred to stepped out, barely making eye contact with her before heading toward the front door.

Gia turned to where Vito stood just inside the office. "What's going on, Vito? Why was the door locked?"

"I think you'd better come inside, Miss Gia," he said quietly. "And lock the door behind you. I have something to tell you that I don't think you want anyone overhearing."

"DAMN IT, I want verification on the name of the shooter," Lucas said to his handler after demanding a one-on-one. This time they'd met at Astoria Park, overlooking the East River. Smith was wearing a city jumpsuit and was pushing a cart that held a garbage bag and a broom. "Which family is he associated with?"

"Calm down, Paretti. Take your cell phone out and pretend you're talking on it. And, for God's sake, turn toward the river away from me. You're being about as subtle as a spurned woman."

"I don't give a damn what I'm being. Gia...I could have been killed this afternoon."

"The shooter wasn't interested in you."

"How can you possibly know that?"

Smith stared at him. "You report to me. Not the other way around. Remember that."

"Trust me. I don't think it's something I'm going to soon forget."

Trying to rein in his anger, Lucas took out his cell phone and then turned toward the East River, staring at the churning waters where countless bodies had been known to float to the surface, not all of them mob related.

"So who's the shooter?"

Smith swept up a crumpled piece of paper, staying true to his temporary undercover character. "Giglio."

"I knew it." Lucas had gotten a brief glimpse of the man, but he had been too far away for him to be sure it was the former Venuto family hit man. "Which family has he signed up with?"

"Well, that's the thing," Smith said quietly. "There's no evidence that he has taken up with another family. In fact, all indicators point to him still working with the Venutos..."

GIA SAT BACK in the office chair staring at the locked door. She was alone in the room now, Vito having left to oversee the lockdown some twenty minutes ago.

But his words still echoed in her mind.

In fact, they were the only words she could seem to concentrate on.

"I hate to tell you this, Gia, but Lucas Paretti is FBI."

She winced as if hearing Vito say the words for the first time all over again.

Her knee-jerk reaction to his statement was to deny that it could be true. She began to defend Luca, tell Vito that she knew him and that never in a million years would he betray her. Not again.

She stopped speaking. In that one moment, she'd held in her hand the final piece of the puzzle she'd been seeking. Where Luca had gone when he'd left the family so long ago. Why not even his parents had appeared capable of contacting him.

And then there was his sudden reappearance and his offer to work for her father a year ago.

Gia's heart beat thickly in her chest as she sat staring at nothing, incapable of movement.

Luca was FBI.

She slowly reviewed everything she'd said to him, everything she'd done with him, in the past two weeks. Considered what he'd uncovered about the family over the past year.

And wished the floor would open up and swallow her whole so she wouldn't have to deal with the complicated questions streaming through her mind.

There was a knock at the door. She ignored it.

"Miss Gia? It's Frankie. I have your coffee. Sorry it took so long, but one of Mr. Cimino's men sent me on an errand and I just got back."

Gia forced herself to get up and go to the door to open it.

Frankie balanced a tray that bore not only coffee, cream and sugar, but also a plate of biscotti.

"Shall I put it on the table?" he asked.

"Yes. Thanks, Frankie."

Gia ordered herself to get her wits together. Too much was going on to give herself over to emotional distress just now. The estate was being locked down and she wasn't sure what all that entailed. Images of metal shutters being closed over the windows and barbed wire being laid out on top of the perimeter fence came to mind.

Then there was the fact that she'd so wholeheartedly believed that Tamburo and the Peluso family had been behind the hit on her father.

But now that Tamburo had been killed…

"Mr. Lorenzo says he'd like to talk to you when you have a minute."

"Yes, well, tell him I don't have a minute. And probably won't until sometime tomorrow," she said absently.

But halfway around the desk she stopped.

"Actually, Frankie, don't worry about it. I'm going to go up and speak to Lorenzo right now."

17

GIA STOOD outside her mother's old room. One of the nurses had left the door ajar. She listened as he berated someone, cursing them and demanding that they provide the medication he needed, that he was in pain.

Gia moved into the room next to her brother's, fingered through the syringes there and then picked up one marked Vitamin B12.

"Sounds like we're not feeling any better than we did this morning," she said upon entering her brother's room.

"That's because we are in extreme pain and our sister has convinced the goddamn doctor that I don't need meds anymore."

She motioned for the harried nurse to leave the room. Gia closed the door after her, her fingers curved around the syringe in her pocket.

"Tamburo's been hit," she said.

"I don't give a shit if the president himself was assassinated. Give me my drugs."

Gia shook her head and leaned against the door with her arms crossed over her chest. "So you don't care that that bullet came during a meeting of all the families? Or that it could have had my name on it?"

Lorenzo looked as if he wanted to shoot her himself. "If it had your name on it, you wouldn't be in here right now torturing me. And I'd have my drugs."

Gia considered what he'd said. During her conversation earlier with his attending physician, she'd learned the symptoms of addiction, all of which Lorenzo displayed. And he'd recommended a course of action. The first of which was to prescribe him the bare minimum of the medications Lorenzo craved. The next was to check him into a facility equipped to handle just such cases.

She didn't want to send Lorenzo away. To do so would be to admit defeat. And would include others in what was essentially a family matter. He was the only true family she had left, but she was ill equipped to see to his needs now, no matter how much she would like to. And he needed to be weaned off the drugs that had turned him into little more than a prescription junkie.

"What happened that day, Lorenzo?" she asked quietly.

He fell instantly quiet and dropped his gaze to

stare at the neatly folded sheet and blanket over his stomach. The black silk pajamas he wore made him appear surprisingly normal, as if he was just a regular guy waking in the morning.

The problem lay in that the bedcovers were a little too neatly folded and it was seven o'clock at night.

Gia stepped nearer the bed, realizing with a start that she had yet to press him for details surrounding his injuries…the same events that had resulted in the deaths of Mario and their father. In the beginning, she was just glad he was still alive and figured that the rest would work itself out in its own time. Once he was well enough, he'd share anything that might help in finding the hit men, and by extension, the person who had hired them.

"I already told you, I don't remember nothing."

"Anything," she automatically corrected, the reminder that she'd always challenged her brothers on their atrocious grammar, stabbing her with nostalgia for times past. "And I don't believe you."

Lorenzo looked at her in surprise, and then the familiar annoyance furrowed his brow. "What else is new? You don't believe that I'm in pain and need my drugs. You don't believe that I can't see to the physical therapy because it hurts too much. You don't believe that I'm capable of making my own decisions about my life."

"That's because if it were left up to you, you'd probably be dead." The comment was a careless, throwaway one. She hadn't meant it.

But his resigned expression told her that she wasn't that far from the mark.

She moved to a chair, suddenly incapable of supporting herself. "Is that what you really wanted? To take your own life?"

"Why the past tense?"

"Tell me those are just words."

Lorenzo didn't respond for a long moment. "You've always been a know-it-all, haven't you? Papa always called you his little miss princess in training for the crown. Before you could talk you would rush into situations battle commander ready to send the troops into action." He shook his head. "I wasn't born with that, you know?" He glanced at her. "Papa said I lacked focus. That women and clubs were all that I had on my mind. He said he kept waiting for me to grow out of it. Fall in love. Marry the right woman. Settle down so I could take more of an interest in the family business. Eventually take over as head of the family one day."

He didn't have to tell Gia the latter. Everyone knew her father had been grooming Lorenzo to take over for him. She hadn't known, however, that her father had had a negative view of Lorenzo's lifestyle or questioned his leadership abilities.

"How did you respond to that?" she asked quietly. "His telling you that you lacked focus?"

Lorenzo stared at her. "How do you think I responded?"

"I don't know or else I wouldn't have asked."

He fell silent again.

Gia determined to wait him out. But after a few minutes, she noticed the way sweat dotted his brow and how he grimaced in pain, and she wondered after a while if he even remembered the original question.

"What happened that day, Lorenzo?" she asked again.

His agitation returned. "Get out of here, Gia. I don't need you passing judgment on me. From what I hear, you haven't been exactly an upright citizen lately."

Her throat tightened. With whom had he been talking about the family's goings-on?

Then she remembered that Vito visited with her brother at least twice a day, sometimes more.

She'd never considered that maybe they talked about business. Mostly because Lorenzo hadn't appeared capable of carrying on a normal conversation.

At least not with her.

"Why would you think I'm passing judgment on you?" she asked.

"Why else would you be in here asking me about something that happened a month and a half ago if you didn't think that I had done something to cause it?"

Gia raised her brows in surprise. "I've never said one thing to give you that impression. I'm merely interested in finding our brother and father's killers and bringing them to justice."

His face darkened.

"Lorenzo? Is there something here I'm missing? Because I'm having a hard time connecting the dots."

His hands began trembling as he fussed with his top blanket. But whether it was because of the scaling back on his pain medication or their conversation, she couldn't be sure.

"Lorenzo?" She got up from the chair and moved closer to his bed, a trembling of her own beginning to shake her from the inside out.

"You just think you know it all, don't you? Me.

Papa. The family." His eyes were accusing, bruised with a pain she suspected surpassed his physical injuries. "You don't know anything, Gia. You don't know anything."

"Then tell me. I want to know, Lorenzo. I need to know." She fought to keep her breathing normal, even. "My life lately has been consumed with finding justice for the loss of our family. I've given up Bona Dea, closed my apartment and moved back out here, tried to take care of a business I had no knowledge of until I was forced to handle it in your stead."

"You really don't have any idea, do you?"

His words were said so softly that she had to lean in closer to hear them.

"Any idea about what?"

He grabbed her arm and she gasped, taken aback by the quick and hard move. "That Tamburo wasn't responsible for the hit against our father."

"Then who was?"

She desperately searched his face for the answer, wanting to shake him in the hopes that it would force it out.

Then the truth struck her. One of the possible truths.

She tried to pull her hand away and he jerked it closer, holding tighter, bruising her skin.

"Ah, now she's beginning to understand."

She watched as his big dark eyes filled with tears, as if all the pain in the world resided there, just beyond their glassy depths.

"Two months ago, Papa gave me a deadline. Told me that I had to shape up and prove myself worthy to play a significant role in the family. And if at the end of that time, I didn't perform to his satisfaction, he was going to look to Mario."

Gia felt the sudden, inexplicable urge to get away, run from the room, to prevent herself from hearing what she feared he was about to say.

"You know what my response was?"

She didn't say anything as hot tears of her own rushed to blur her vision.

"I asked if you know what my response was?" he said louder, jerking her wrist again.

Gia winced and shook her head.

"I said, 'yes, Papa.' Just like every other time he tried to fill my head with advice and guidance, pushing me in a direction I didn't want to go."

"Where did you want to go?" she whispered.

"I wanted to be a painter. Did you know that, Gia? Did anyone in the family know that I have a studio downtown? That a local gallery had just offered to spotlight my work? Had set the date for my first official showing?"

Gia blinked, remembering that he had liked to draw when they were younger, and that he used to make off with her sketch pads from time to time. She'd thought that it was because he'd liked to torment her. Normal sibling-rivalry stuff.

She'd never expected that he'd actually used the pads.

"I told Papa, and you know what he did? He gave me the ultimatum. Told me art was for gays and that I'd better get my act together or he'd cut me off from the family."

The trembling in Gia's stomach moved outward so that her knees felt suddenly weak.

"So I did the only thing I knew how to do. The only thing he'd taught me."

Gia began shaking her head, trying to ward off the coming words.

"I conspired to get rid of him."

"No!" She thought she'd screamed the word, but instead it came out as a barely hushed whisper.

"Yes, Gia. I helped kill our own father. I mapped out the route we would take out that day to meet with the Guarino brothers. Scheduled down to the minute exactly where we would be, and when. So when the gunmen pulled up on either side of our car, the only one who wasn't surprised was me."

Gia tried to jerk her wrist from his grasp again. "Let me go!" she demanded. "Goddamn it, release me."

"Why? So you can do what I've wanted to do since that day? Since the moment I watched our father take that first bullet in the arm?" He squeezed his eyes shut and his grip tightened. "I don't think I'll ever forget his face. The way he looked at me. I don't know how he knew, but…he did. He stared at me in shock, as if the last thing he would have expected was for me to want him dead."

"Stop it! I don't want to hear any more."

He hauled her closer. "Then give me the goddamn drugs, Gia," he said viciously. "Let me end this terrible…suffering. Let me kill myself and stop the pain."

THE SUN WAS HANGING low on the horizon as Lucas sped up the curving driveway to the Trainello house. His every nerve ending was on alert. His every instinct told him that something was going horribly wrong.

He climbed from the car, his rushed steps slowing as he realized that there were no other cars to be seen. No armed men.

He hurried up to the door and opened it, surprised to find it unlocked and with no one in the foyer.

"Gia?" he called out.

His own voice echoed back at him.

Jesus. What was going on?

He covered the first floor in ten seconds flat, finding no one there. Not in the library, Gia's office, the kitchen. The place was completely empty.

He took the steps upwards two at a time, his heart racing in his chest. What was going on? Where had everyone gone? Where were Vito and his men? Why wasn't the place being guarded?

Where was Gia?

He threw open the door to her bedroom and stood staring inside. Relief flushed through his system. Gia was curled up on top of her bed in a fetal position, ignorant to the world.

The next emotion he knew was fear…

18

GIA VAGUELY HEARD Luca's voice calling out for her, but she was unable to respond, incapable of even the simplest movement. She lay on her bed, longing to close her eyes, but even that small relief was denied her because every time she blinked, a series of unwanted images branded the back of her eyelids.

Vito's face when he'd told her that Luca was an FBI agent…

Lorenzo's brutal grip on her hand as he confessed to having killed their father and brother…

The imagined expression on her father's face when he realized his own son was responsible for killing him…

She heard her bedroom door open and crash against the inside wall.

"Gia."

The one word was said in relief, and almost immediately she felt Luca's weight on the bed beside her.

She finally found the strength to move. Away from him.

"Don't," she whispered, rolling over and sitting on the opposite side of the bed, her back to him.

She felt his hand on her shoulder, warmth spreading through her blouse and over her skin. She didn't shrug him off.

"What's is it, Gia? What's the matter?"

Where did she start? With the fact that her entire life over the past six weeks had been a lie? Beginning with her desire to make some stranger pay for the loss of two members of her family only to discover that her last remaining family member, her blood, had been the one who had virtually pulled the trigger?

And ending with Luca's ultimate betrayal?

"Tell me what in the hell is going on." Luca grasped her shoulders and forced her to face him in the middle of the bed. She glared at him as if she'd like nothing more but to see him dead.

He blinked in the face of her nonverbal confrontation. Then his hands slowly dropped onto the mattress and his shoulders slumped.

"You know," he said simply.

Gia swallowed past the Long Island-size lump in her throat. She nodded. She knew.

In fact, she was afraid that she knew too much.

Her brain hurt from the infusion of so much unwanted information.

Her heart felt as if it was about to explode in her chest.

"Gia, I…"

She finally looked up into his face, wanting, needing so badly to hear something that might give her the tiniest bit of hope.

"I know there's no way I can possibly make this up to you. Just know that this…my assignment…had nothing to do with you."

"But it had to do with my father."

He didn't say anything for a long moment, and then he nodded. "Yes, it did."

"Why? What did my father ever do to you that he deserved your spite? Your hate?"

His eyes shot blue flames. "He killed my brother."

She blinked at him, his words stealing the breath from her lungs.

"Not directly. He didn't pull the trigger. But he created the environment that made Angelo a victim of a violent crime that wouldn't have existed had there been no mob."

"Your brother was mugged," she whispered.

"By rival family members who were competing against Angelo for the same numbers business."

Frustrated rage filled her from toe to head. "Guns don't kill people, Luca. People kill people."

"If you want to throw platitudes my way, how about the one that says 'the buck stops here?' The trail of bucks in this case ended in your father's hand. And in the hand of every egomaniacal mafia family head in this city and every other city."

"And what makes you think you're better than any one of them?"

LUCAS STARED AT her, her question catching him up short.

She had him there. And if someone had made the same query seven years ago, he may never have chosen the path he had.

But what about the alternative? Would he have gone on to become a lawyer for the mob? Spent the past seven years repping the thugs that thrived on bloodshed and violence? Would he have crossed the line and given into blood-lust himself?

But most important, would he and Gia have gotten married, had the baby she'd been pregnant with, the first of many?

The pain that was reflected on her face tore at his own heart.

A sound outside caught his attention. Alarm swept through him as he went to the window and looked out. The sun had almost completely set.

Why did he sense it was a countdown of sorts?

"Gia, where is everyone?"

She shifted on the bed and ran her hand through her tousled hair. "What?"

He looked at her over his shoulder. "Vito? The family goons? Where are they?"

She got up from the bed to stand next to him, going out of her way not to touch him as she stared out the window at the quiet grounds. "I sent Frankie back to the stables earlier."

"No one's here, Gia. There are no cars in the driveway, no one around anywhere. Even the housekeeper appears to be gone."

She looked at him in unease.

"Oh, God," she whispered.

"Come on." He grasped her arm and led her out into the hall and then down the stairs. She looked around as they moved, as surprised as he had been at the utter silence.

The automatic floodlights outside the house switched on in the waning daylight, the only source of illumination inside the house. Lucas paused in the foyer, gripping Gia's hand so tightly she made a small, muffled sound.

"Sorry," he said, lessening his grip. "We need to get out of here."

"Lorenzo…" Gia whispered.

"We'll send an ambulance for him."

"No, that's not what I meant. I mean…"

Her words drifted off and he waited for her to continue.

Her dark eyes welled with tears.

Lucas drew her closer, praying she wouldn't refuse his touch. "What is it?" he murmured.

"My father's own son conspired to kill him," she said so quietly he nearly didn't make out her words.

"Who told you that?"

"Lorenzo, himself."

He pulled her fully into his arms. "Oh, Gia. I'm so, so sorry."

It made a twisted kind of sense once he heard it. Over the past year he'd watched father and son butt heads more times than he could count. Giovanni had wanted to see Lorenzo step up to the proverbial plate, and Lorenzo kept kicking the dirt as if the last thing he wanted to do was take a swing at any ball his father threw his way.

"He didn't do it alone, Gia," he told her, the scent of her sweet-smelling hair filling his senses.

"What do you mean?" She drew back to look at him.

"I mean that while he may have helped, he wasn't the power behind the trigger."

"But Tamburo…"

He shook his head. "The Peluso family didn't have anything to do with this. None of the other families did."

She appeared not to be following him.

"Giglio hit Tamburo at the meeting today. And he wasn't working on behalf of any of the other families," he told her.

She searched his eyes. "But if Giglio wasn't working for someone else, then…"

She trailed off and then her face went pale.

"Vito," she said in a hushed whisper.

Lucas held on to her tightly as she laid her head against his chest, seemingly powerless to stop herself, seeking comfort from any source that wouldn't cause her hurt.

"Don't worry, Gia. We'll get him." He kissed the top of her head, smoothing his hand over her back. "But…"

"But what?"

"But I'm going to have to ask for your cooperation."

Her expression turned stony. "You mean rat Vito out to the feds?"

He let his gaze linger on her lush lips. "Do you hate me, Gia?"

She didn't say anything for a long moment. Then, finally, "No, Luca. I could never hate you."

"Look, I don't know what other choice we have. The way I see it, everyone you trusted has turned on you. If we don't get Vito first…"

He didn't have to finish his sentence. They both knew what would happen if they didn't stop Vito. He wouldn't stop until he got them.

"Come on," he said, grasping her hand. "Let's get out of here."

He began moving toward the door when Gia stood stock-still. "I think it's already too late."

GIA CAUGHT a beam of light that wasn't connected to the spotlights outside. It swept the front lawn and then pierced the sheer curtains on the front window. Luca spotted it at the same time she did and yanked her back just as the flashlight would have caught her legs.

Somewhere out back the dogs barked loudly.

"Damn!" Luca let go of her hand and took his cell phone out of his pocket while she tried to figure out how many might be outside.

The phone beeped oddly. Luca cursed and continued to try to dial out. It beeped again.

He flicked it closed. "They must have a jamming device set up so we can't call out. I might be able to catch a signal from an upper floor."

"What about the hard line?" Gia asked.

"If they jammed the cell frequency, they most certainly cut that."

The flashlight beam swept the foyer again and this time Gia pulled him away from it.

There was a brief, shrill canine shriek and then suddenly the barking stopped.

Gia's heart beat an unsteady rhythm in her chest, heightened by the adrenaline pumping through her veins.

The mafia had taken away her entire family. And now they were trying to kill her.

"Gia, we—"

She grabbed the front of Luca's shirt in both her hands. "Can I trust you?"

He stared at her as if the last thing he would have expected was her question. "With your life."

"No, Lucas, I mean, can I trust you. Really trust you?"

"Tell me what you want me to do."

19

LUCAS FOLLOWED Gia to the office only to find the door locked, the key she tried to open it with refusing to work. The enclosed hallway protected them from anyone outside.

It would prove a gauntlet if anyone was inside.

"Vito must have changed the locks and security code."

Lucas couldn't claim full knowledge of the estate, but he guessed that Giovanni's old office would have proven a refuge of sorts, most likely more secure than any other room in the house. It was centrally located and had probably been reinforced with bulletproof glass and door.

"What about the basement?" he asked.

Gia shook her head. "No. Come on."

She led the way back toward the foyer, being careful about possible watchful eyes, and then went into the library. With frantic movements, she ran her hands along a line of books and then pulled one out on the upper left-hand shelf. Nothing happened. She continued with a succession of books.

"Come on, come on, where is it?"

Lucas was about to ask what she was looking for, when he heard a click and the middle section of the bookcase swung outward, knocking a few leather-bound novels to the floor.

He'd worked there for over a year and had never known a secret door existed.

Then again, he was coming to understand that there were a lot of things he didn't know about.

He followed Gia through the doorway, where she pressed a button and the bookshelf closed behind them with a loud, metallic click. Another button and the twelve-by-twelve-foot hidden room was illuminated by a fluorescent light fixture on the ceiling.

"Christ, what is this?"

"Dad had the room built when he bought the place. He showed it to us kids when we were young, told us if anything ever happened, we were to make our way here where we'd be safe. He even held fire drills of sorts. Whoever was the first to get here got his or her choice of gelato."

She busily typed on a keyboard that sat on a shelf before a dozen television monitors.

"Then Vito would know about it," Lucas pointed out.

She stared at him. "No, he wouldn't. Papa trusted a lot of people, but he trusted no one completely. Including Vito."

"Wouldn't Lorenzo have said something?"

She blanched. "I don't see why he would have. He seems preoccupied with his own sins right now. Let's hope that isn't one of them. And if he should tell him now, it would be too late." She knocked on the wall. "The room is encased in twelve inches of steel. There are three separate air sources in case any should be blocked. And should the outside air be unusable…"

She pointed toward a series of metal cabinet doors to her left.

Lucas opened the first and found canister upon canister of oxygen as well as gas masks and bodysuits.

When he turned, he found that the monitors in front of Gia had lit up.

"Here we go."

Lucas moved to stand behind her, watching as images from all the security cameras placed inside the house popped up. Cameras he hadn't even been aware of. One after another she scrolled through them. The foyer, the kitchen, the library, only the office didn't show. He supposed that Giovanni hadn't wanted the interior of his office broadcast over a closed-circuit television system. Smart man.

"They're not inside yet," Gia said almost to herself. "Let's see what's going on outside…"

Another few keystrokes and the images changed.

And what they revealed caused her to stand upright and take a step back from the console, bumping into Lucas. He put his arms around her.

"My God, there must be at least a dozen of them out there."

Lucas had to agree. And those were only the ones they could see.

Twenty feet out, men in camouflage crouched or hid behind bushes, each of them using their weapon sights and flashlights strapped to the top to scan the exterior of the house and what they could make out of the interior. They looked like a paramilitary team instead of mafia hit men. And they were all armed to the teeth.

If he didn't know better, he'd think that an official tactical team was bearing down on the house.

But he did know better, because Smith was waiting for him to give the signal. And he couldn't give it.

Besides, he knew that many of the young men

now serving in the mafia army had also served in the U.S. Army. And that bootcamplike operations had been set up in upstate New York primarily for the training of the new wave of mob soldiers.

"What are we going to do?" Gia whispered.

THE ROOM SHOULD have made Gia feel safe. But as she tried to keep track of all the men outside methodically advancing on the house, she instead felt like a mouse caught in a trap.

"Is there any way to get a line outside?" Luca asked.

She turned to face him. Strangely, the betrayal she'd felt earlier had fled, flushed away by the urgency of their situation. "I don't know. I think there's a separate phone line that runs into the room…"

As she talked, she scanned the small room. She found a telephone handset in a cradle on the wall next to the monitors. She picked it up. Nothing. She punched a couple of buttons on the base. Still, nothing.

"Looks like your father was expecting WWIII."

Gia turned toward where Luca had opened the other cabinet doors. Arms of all shapes and sizes were racked and sorted along with boxes of ammunition. Luca took out a semiautomatic rifle, checked the chamber and then quickly loaded it. He put it aside, picked up a pistol, and then exchanged the empty clip for a fresh one. That one he tucked into the back waist of his pants.

The sight of him looking so comfortable around guns made her wonder if she knew him at all. Yes, while he'd been associated with the family seven years ago, her father had kept him close, his going to law school exempting him from the most criminal jobs.

No, he hadn't picked up his arms skills from the family. He'd learned them from the FBI.

"You're not thinking about trying to fight them off," she whispered.

He loaded another pistol and held it out to her. She didn't move. He took her hand and placed the cold, heavy metal in her palm. "What do you suggest? That we hide in here until they all go away?"

"Why not? They'll search the house, find no one here…"

She trailed off, realizing there was one person there: Lorenzo.

"We need to move your brother to the safe room," he said as if he'd read her mind. "Before they breach the house."

"How do we do that?"

He turned back toward the cabinets, taking out a headset and a handheld radio. "I'm going out. You're going to keep me informed via radio."

"But it won't work through the steel."

He looked at her meaningfully. "We're going to have to leave the door open."

Gia felt sick to her stomach. But it had to be done. The camera in her brother's room showed him alone and sleeping. And she couldn't find a sign of any of his nurses anywhere. Either they had caught wind of what was going down, or they'd been warned by one of Vito's men to leave.

Only, she'd been so obsessed with her emotions she hadn't realized that while her inner world and everything she thought she understood was crashing down around her ears, the outer world was, too.

Gia met Luca's gaze. "If you're going to do it, you'd better do it now."

He cut the lights, the monitors casting an eerie blue glow around the room, and moved to open the door.

Gia caught his arm and turned him toward her, looking up into his eyes. She couldn't think of anything to say. And since he wasn't saying anything to respond to, she did the only thing she could think of to show how she felt: she kissed him.

She'd swung through so many extremes that afternoon. The meeting where Tamburo was killed and she'd been in fear for her own life even as she tried to ascertain who was responsible for robbing her father of his. Returning home to Vito's revelation that the man she loved was out to destroy her family. Seeking details from her only blood relative left in Lorenzo only to find out he'd been the one who'd wanted their father dead. Then discovering that Uncle Vito, her father's most loyal friend, had not only betrayed him, he'd betrayed her, working in concert with her brother in order to gain control over the Venuto family.

And now, the realization that family wasn't about a collection of those who shared the same lineage, went to the same church or were born of the same parents.

Family was love.

And she loved Luca Paretti with every ounce of her being.

And she trusted him the same way.

She finally broke off the kiss and stroked his cheek with her fingers. "Be careful."

"You do the same. You see anyone coming in the monitors, close that door, do you hear me?"

She nodded, hating to send him out there alone. Hating that she was going to be alone and exposed.

But there was no other choice. Even though Lorenzo had been in on their father's killing, she couldn't just leave him lying there, vulnerable to the gunmen moving ever closer to the house where they'd waste no time gaining access.

Her father might be dead. But her brother was still alive. And it was not her job to judge him. That would come when he stood facing St. Peter at heaven's gate. And she'd prefer his journey there be a natural one, after a long life spent considering his sins and trying to make amends for them.

"You're clear," she said into the radio, watching as the men outside were still a good few feet away from the front of the house. "But you don't have much time. Go up the stairs. Now!"

He did as she ordered. She switched monitors to watch him hurry down the second-floor hall, his handgun stretched out in front of him.

He was in her brother's room in no time.

Gia sagged slightly in relief.

Her mother's old bedroom looked strange in the fishbowl view that allowed the camera to take in most of the area. The bed that dominated it looked extralarge, and Luca seemed to grow as he got closer to it. In the dark, everything appeared in various shades of black and white and gray.

She watched as Luca tucked his pistol into the back waist of his pants and neared the bed. Only, Lorenzo wasn't waking up.

And then a third person entered the picture from the far corner.

"Luca!" she cried into the radio. "Behind you!"

20

LUCAS REACHED FOR his pistol and turned around at the same time so that he was holding his gun on none other than Vito Cimino.

The older man had his own weapon trained on him.

"Weaknesses," Vito said, his smile flashing in the semidarkness, only the outside floodlights relieving the shadows. "It's important in this business that you know everyone's weaknesses."

Lucas glanced quickly at Lorenzo, not feeling good about how still he was.

"I knew Gia would come after her brother. All I had to do was stay here and wait. Little did I know that she'd send you to do the job for her. Maybe the girl's smarter than I gave her credit for."

Lucas narrowed his gaze on him. "How long have you known I was with the FBI?"

Vito shrugged, stepping closer. "Since you signed on. That was part of my job, checking out new personnel." He looked pleased with himself. And well he should, because Lucas and Smith had done everything they could to cover their tracks. "The feds think they're so smart. They have guys planted here, planted there. What they don't know is that we have a few of our guys planted with them." He made a satisfied sound. "Looks like you would have been better off cleaning your own house before coming into this one."

"Why did you keep the information to yourself?"

"Because my plan to take my rightful place as head of the Venuto family was already well under way. And just like it's important that I know my opponent's weaknesses—in Giovanni's case it was his children—it's equally important to know when to use those same weaknesses against them." He shrugged again. "Besides, I knew the family didn't have anything to worry about when it came to you. Giovanni was already being shown the door, so it wasn't difficult to talk Claudio into slamming it shut behind him…permanently. And you always did have a soft spot for Gia."

Lucas heard Gia's voice in his ear.

"Two just gained access to the front," she said.

"Close the door," he said. "Close the door now!"

He ripped off his headset in case she chose to stay in contact with him over protecting herself. He tossed it to the bed, only then seeing the spot of red against the white blanket. A spot that grew wider.

It was then that he realized that Lorenzo wasn't sleeping. He was dead.

GIA CURSED Luca for taking off his headset and then pushed the button to close the safe-room door even as she kept her gaze glued to the scene unfolding. Vito was only a couple of feet away from Luca now.

"So tell me, Vito," Luca said to the other man. "How is it you think yourself deserving to be head of the Venuto family?"

Gia hated that she could hear what was being said but that she couldn't respond.

"Kill him!" she ordered Luca. "Just shoot him, for God's sake, and get back here."

She glanced at the other monitors. Another man had gained access to the kitchen.

But wait…

She looked closer. He didn't look like the other men. He didn't appear to be armed and he wasn't wearing a mask.

Her stomach lurched. Frankie.

What was he still doing there? Could he be in on what was going down? Or had he been in his room in the stables, saw movement in the house and made his way over? It would be just like him to not see the men even now making their way closer to the back of the house. Then again, the place was always teeming with armed men, so why should these be any different?

Oh, God.

The kid was lucky he had made it to the house in one piece. But how long would that luck hold out once the gunmen gained access and started shooting at anything that moved?

She smacked the hand-size button that controlled the door. It opened with a low, electronic hum. Gia began to slip into the library, then backtracked and picked up two handguns, shoving one into the front of her slacks, holding the other straight out in front of her.

"Frankie!" she whispered fiercely. "It's me. Gia. I'm in the library."

"Hey, Miss Gia. What's going on? How come none of the lights are working? All of them are on outside—"

His words were sheared off by the sound of a bullet shattering the glass of the kitchen door.

"Frankie, run!"

He headed in the opposite direction.

"No, toward me! Here in the library."

He stopped, apparently unsure which way to turn, and then finally started toward the library…just as the library doors shattered inward.

LUCAS'S PALMS were dry where he held his gun steady on Vito, although his adrenaline levels shot up at the sound of breaking glass coming from downstairs.

Damn!

Had Gia closed the door to the safe room? Was she even now inside, watching everything unfold on the monitors?

Or had she left the door open and was now prey to the men who were gaining entrance to the house?

Nowhere in his mind was how he was going to make it back to the room.

"Why did you kill Lorenzo?" he demanded of Vito. "He was no threat to you."

"He was more threat than you know."

"Because he conspired with you to kill his father?"

Vito stared at him.

"Yes, Gia and I know. Lorenzo told her this afternoon."

"No matter. He was of no use to me anymore, anyway. And just as soon as I get you and Gia out of the way, the family's mine, no challenge anywhere."

"Oh, but there will be challenge everywhere, won't there, Vito? Because that's the nature of this business. The last man standing is the king of the hill."

He pulled the trigger at the same time as he ducked away from the bed. The bullet hit Vito in the upper chest. The older man stumbled back a few feet, but he remained standing. Lucas hit the floor with a thud and scrambled to a crouched position, his gun still out. Vito's wound wasn't immediately fatal. But judging by the amount of blood spreading across his chest, it might kill him soon.

"You son of a bitch!" Vito shouted, pressing one hand over the wound while he aimed his weapon with his other.

Lucas pulled his trigger again, this time aiming for Vito's head. He hit him in the forehead with deadly accuracy.

Why take any chances?

GIA WAS AS LOW to the floor as she could be and still be mobile. She held the gun out with both hands. "Here! Over here by the bookcase," she called to Frankie.

The teen ran in her direction and at the moment she knew hope that they'd both make it inside the safe room with no problem.

Unfortunately others apparently heard her call out and a line of automatic gunfire embedded bullets in the wall to her right, splinters from the wood paneling filling the air. Frankie got hit in the calf and fell immediately to his knees, only a few feet away.

Gia put her gun down, her firepower no match for the weapons the others had. She hurried toward the young man.

"Come on, damn it!" she whispered harshly. "It's only a few feet. You can make it."

"I don't know, Miss Gia," Frankie said, his voice sounding unusually raspy. "I don't think I can."

She grabbed him under the arms from the back, determined to drag him if she had to.

More gunfire. She moved as fast as she could. She dropped to her knees, protected by the open safe-room door.

"Wow, Miss Gia. I didn't know it would hurt so bad…"

His words trailed off, but they were enough to let her know he was still, somehow, miraculously, alive. She stumbled to her feet again and pulled. Only a foot and a half to go.

"Hang in there, kiddo. Hang in there."

The sound of footsteps on crunching glass. She blinked up to find one of the masked men standing ten feet away, his weapon aimed directly at her.

A single shot. Only she wasn't the one who was hit. Instead, the bullet hit Frankie in the upper left chest.

Tears welled in her eyes and her heart threatened to beat straight out of her chest as she turned to dive toward the room, hoping against hope that the automatic door would close in time to save her.

Another shadow appeared behind the gunman. Luca!

Only it wasn't Luca. She recognized him as Carlo Giglio, the hit man who had once worked for her father and who had taken Tamburo out under Vito's direction earlier that afternoon.

Her feet slipped against something wet. Her hope beginning to wane, she realized it was Frankie's blood that coated the polished wood floor.

So this was it. This was how it was going to happen. She was going to die mere inches away from a room that would have shielded her from a thousand bullets. In her father's house. The place where she had grown up. The last of the Trainellos gunned down in cold blood.

Everything seemed to move in slow motion. Her right foot caught traction and she lunged at the same time she heard the dull echo of another bullet exiting its chamber.

Only it wasn't the gunman who had fired. It was Giglio. And he had been aiming not for her, but the back of the head of the gunman.

21

"I'M GOING IN," Lucas said into his cell phone, talking to Smith. Lucas had managed to scramble out of the bedroom window and climbed to the roof where he had gained cell access, pressing the panic button by uttering a single word to his handler: "Firefly."

Five minutes later, Smith was there, and helicopters hovered above the estate, illuminating the entire area with light. FBI tactical agents were dropping by rope to the ground. Bright flashes lit the night as gunfire erupted.

"Don't make a move, Paretti!" Smith ordered him.

Lucas dropped his phone and climbed back down and through the same bedroom window. Moving past both Lorenzo's and Vito's bodies, he grabbed Vito's extra gun and then headed for the hall, not stopping until he'd run down the stairs, through the foyer and into the library. He needed to make sure Gia had closed the door. That she was sitting safe in the room, cut off from all that was going on around her.

The sight of a body on the floor stopped him in his tracks. Oh God. Not again...

His heart threatened to go into arrest.

He slowly neared the still form lying on the floor, releasing his held breath when he realized it wasn't Gia's body, but Frankie's.

He reached down and searched for a pulse in the kid's slender neck.

The hidden door began to open. As soon as it was wide enough, he slid in sideways and gathered Gia up into his arms, kissing her face even as he pressed the button to close the door again behind him.

"Sweet Jesus, I thought that was you outside," he said harshly, holding her so tightly he was afraid he was hurting her.

"It's Frankie. I tried to help him, tried to get him inside, but...I couldn't. I just couldn't."

He tunneled both hands into her hair and held her cheek against his, feeling the hot dampness of her tears on hers. "Thank God that you're okay," he murmured harshly. "Frankie's still alive. We have to get him help now."

It was then he became aware that they weren't alone in the room.

Instantly, he shoved Gia aside and drew the weapon he had tucked in the back of his pants at the same time as the other man did the same.

Giglio.

"Stop," Gia shouted. "Stop right now, both of you."

Lucas looked between Gia and the hit man, trying to fit the pieces together.

"He saved my life," she said, looking like she had been to hell and back. There were wood chips in her hair, smears on her face, and blood all but covered her hands where she hadn't completely wiped them clean. He guessed it was Frankie's blood.

"I'll lose mine if you lose yours," the toughened gunman said.

"I don't understand," Lucas said to Gia.

Despite his offer, Giglio dislodged his left hand from his weapon and held it up. A moment later, he dropped his gun to the floor and held up his other hand.

"Ain't no big deal," Giglio said.

"But you killed Tamburo." Lucas kept his gun on him.

"Yeah, I did. But I thought I was doing it on behalf of Gia. That's what Vito led me to believe." He looked down at his large hands. Lucas wondered if he saw all the blood that covered the deceptively clean skin. "It wasn't until a few minutes ago that I realized that Vito had lied to me. Lied to all the men. It wasn't Gia he was trying to protect. It was her he was trying to kill." His head snapped upright, and eyes that were amazingly green and alert looked at Lucas. "Giovanni Trainello was like a father to me. I would never have betrayed him to nobody." He nodded toward Gia. "Even though she don't know me, she's like a sister to me. I couldn't stand by and let someone kill her. I vowed that I'd protect the Venuto family to the death. And to me, the Trainello family has always been the Venuto family. Ain't nothing going to change that. Ever."

Lucas finally lowered his gun.

The world was sometimes a strange place. Gia's real brother, Lorenzo, had plotted to kill their father.

And a jaded hit man she didn't even know had put his own life on the line for hers.

Gia moved back into his arms and he held her, just thanking God that she was okay.

And she was okay, wasn't she? Even with the FBI taking out the attackers outside, and with them safely closed up in the room, she wasn't avoiding him, grabbing on to his status as FBI as a reason to push him away. Instead she clutched to him as if he was the most important person in her life.

He pulled her away slightly so he could look into her eyes, seeing in them the love that had always been there. A little dented, a bit shadowed by betrayal, and tried by fire, but love nonetheless. Love for him.

He kissed her deeply, feeling his own love for her balloon within him.

Everything was going to be okay. He knew that as certainly as he knew his own name. So long as Gia loved him, everything was going to be all right.

Epilogue

Three years later...

THE OLD TRAINELLO ESTATE couldn't have looked more different. But the changes weren't about aesthetics. Rather, the family that lived there now shared little in common with the crime family that had once inhabited it.

Mostly.

Gia Trainello Paretti stood at the kitchen counter that was covered with flour and rolled out fresh pasta. She methodically cut ravioli squares, filling half with ground beef and tomato, the other with a mix of ricotta, Romano and Parmesan cheese.

It sometimes seemed impossible that three years had passed since the night that had changed her life forever...and then at times it seemed decades ago. Every now and again, she still jolted awake in the middle of the night, drenched in a cold sweat, convinced that an army of gunmen was advancing on the house. But then Luca, her husband and father to their two-year-old son, Angelo, would cradle her in his arms, and she would know that no one hid outside waiting to catch her in the crosshairs of their scope.

The reason for that was twofold. First, she and Luca had called for a final meeting with the remaining three heads of the crime families a week after Vito's failed takeover attempt. Through sometimes heated negotiations, and due to more than a bit of Luca's persuasive bargaining powers, they'd brokered a deal that dissolved, once and for all, the Venuto crime family.

All illegal activities had been divided between the three families. Legal businesses with questionable side activities were sold to the highest bidders.

And Gia disavowed any right to the Venuto family name or any activities that might be carried out now or at any time in the future on behalf of the same.

The second reason she felt secure in the knowledge that she was no longer at risk was her husband.

She smiled wistfully now as she dropped the ravioli one by one into a large pot of boiling water. Luca was not only the man she'd always loved, and would always love, no matter what, she knew that he would give his very life in order to save hers. And she would do the same for him.

And with the addition of little Angelo into their lives, nine months exactly after the date of their erotic encounter on the kitchen counter, both of them would do the same for their son.

Luca was no longer with the FBI. While he didn't go into detail about the explanation behind his resignation from the bureau, she suspected it had something to do with her, and the FBI's wish to bring her up on charges. Charges they couldn't file because Luca refused to turn state's evidence.

So she'd given up being the Lady Boss, and he'd given up his badge. An equitable compromise, she thought.

Now he commuted into the city via the train three days a week to work as an estate attorney, and she worked as a freelance designer for Bona Dea.

Gia felt a vague pang in her chest. If every now and again she felt a bit of sorrow that her father's hard work and sacrifices—including his life—in order to keep the business that was the Venuto family going strong were lost, all she had to do was look into Angelo's bright blue eyes to know that she'd made the right decision.

So much bloodshed. So much innocence lost.

The mafia family might be about connections. But love of her blood family trumped all. She would do anything and everything in order to keep them safe. And that meant keeping them out of harm's way.

If every now and again the widow of an ex-family member showed up on their doorstep needing help, and she extended that help, that was between her and the widow. No one else need know about it.

She caught herself absently running her hand over her slightly rounded stomach and looked down at her apron-covered baby bump.

The sound of laughter caught her attention and she looked out the window to where their two-year-old son giggled in delight as he toddled under the spray of the hose.

Hands lightly grasped her hips from behind and Luca pressed his body against hers. She tilted her head to give him access to her neck and he kissed it. "Mmm, something smells good."

"I'm making ravioli."

"That's not what I was talking about."

Angelo's laughter sounded again and they looked through the window together at where the toddler was swept into large, male hands and held up in the sunlight.

Carlo Giglio.

Luca shook his head. "Who would have thought a man with his past would be so gentle with a child?"

Angelo squealed in delight and Carlo's pock-marked face broke into a wide grin as he swung the boy around like an airplane, instructing him to extend his arms and even making zooming sounds as Frankie stood nearby, watching affectionately. The kid still needed considerable physical therapy but everything pointed to his making a full recovery. And he and the old hit man had formed a close bond with Carlo taking the younger man under his wing and leading him in a direction well away from the one he'd chosen at the same age.

Gia couldn't imagine her family being complete without both of them in it.

Okay, Gia thought, so maybe the fact that Giglio insisted on staying on at the house as their head of security had a little to do with her feeling safe when she woke up in those cold sweats. After all, there was a difference between ignorance and preparedness.

She turned from the stove to drape her arms around her husband's neck and kiss him deeply, staring into eyes that reflected the love that expanded in her own chest. Besides, could anybody anywhere ever say they were completely safe? The key was to do as much as you could, and then live every moment as if it was your last.

Because it very well could be.

* * * * *

SPECIAL EDITION®

LIFE, LOVE AND FAMILY

These contemporary romances will strike a chord with you as heroines juggle life and relationships on their way to true love.

New York Times *bestselling author Linda Lael Miller brings you a* BRAND-NEW *contemporary story featuring her fan-favorite McKettrick family.*

Meg McKettrick is surprised to be reunited with her high school flame, Brad O'Balli-van. After enjoying a career as a country-and-western singer, Brad aches for a home and family…and seeing Meg again makes him realize he still loves her. But their pride manages to interfere with love…until an unexpected matchmaker gets involved.

Turn the page for a sneak preview of
THE McKETTRICK WAY
by Linda Lael Miller
On sale November 20.
wherever books are sold.

Brad shoved the truck into gear and drove to the bottom of the hill, where the road forked. Turn left, and he'd be home in five minutes. Turn right, and he was headed for Indian Rock.

He had no damn business going to Indian Rock.

He had nothing to say to Meg McKettrick, and if he never set eyes on the woman again, it would be two weeks too soon.

He turned right.

He couldn't have said why.

He just drove straight to the Dixie Dog Drive-In.

Back in the day, he and Meg used to meet at the Dixie Dog, by tacit agreement, when either of them had been away. It had been some kind of universe thing, purely intuitive.

Passing familiar landmarks, Brad told himself he ought to turn around. The old days were gone. Things had ended badly between him and Meg anyhow, and she wasn't going to be at the Dixie Dog.

He kept driving.

He rounded a bend, and there was the Dixie Dog. Its big neon sign, a giant hot dog, was all lit up and going through its corny sequence—first it was covered in red squiggles of light, meant to suggest ketchup, and then yellow, for mustard.

Brad pulled into one of the slots next to a speaker, rolled down the truck window and ordered.

A girl roller-skated out with the order about five minutes later.

When she wheeled up to the driver's window, smiling, her eyes went wide with recognition, and she dropped the tray with a clatter.

Silently Brad swore. Damn if he hadn't forgotten he was a famous country singer.

The girl, a skinny thing wearing too much eye makeup, immediately started to cry. "I'm sorry!" she sobbed, squatting to gather up the mess.

"It's okay," Brad answered quietly, leaning to look down at her, catching a glimpse of her plastic name tag. "It's okay, Mandy. No harm done."

"I'll get you another dog and a shake right away, Mr. O'Ballivan!"

"Mandy?"

She stared up at him pitifully, sniffling. Thanks to the copious tears, most of the goop on her eyes had slid south. "Yes?"

"When you go back inside, could you not mention seeing me?"

"But you're Brad O'Ballivan!"

"Yeah," he answered, suppressing a sigh. "I know."

She rolled a little closer. "You wouldn't happen to have a picture you could autograph for me, would you?"

"Not with me," Brad answered.

"You could sign this napkin, though," Mandy said. "It's only got a little chocolate on the corner."

Brad took the paper napkin and her order pen, and scrawled his name. Handed both items back through the window.

She turned and whizzed back toward the side entrance to the Dixie Dog.

Brad waited, marveling that he hadn't considered incidents like this one before he'd decided to come back home. In retrospect, it seemed shortsighted, to say the least, but the truth was, he'd expected to be—Brad O'Ballivan.

Presently Mandy skated back out again, and this time she managed to hold on to the tray.

"I didn't tell a soul!" she whispered. "But Heather and Darlene *both* asked me why my mascara was all smeared." Efficiently she hooked the tray onto the bottom edge of the window.

Brad extended payment, but Mandy shook her head.

"The boss said it's on the house, since I dumped your first order on the ground."

He smiled. "Okay, then. Thanks."

Mandy retreated, and Brad was just reaching for the food when a bright red Blazer whipped into the space beside his. The driver's door sprang open, crashing into the metal speaker, and somebody got out in a hurry.

Something quickened inside Brad.

And in the next moment Meg McKettrick was standing practically on his running board, her blue eyes blazing.

Brad grinned. "I guess you're not over me after all," he said.